WA

Wake Up, It's Midnight! is the second book in the Naitabal Mystery series. The other titles in the series *are Danger, Keep Out!; Wild Woods, Dark Secret; Behind Locked Doors; Ghost Island* and *Dead Man's Chest.*

NAITABAL:	A wild species of human, aged about ten.
NAITABAL OAK:	An oak tree suitable for habitation by Naitabals.
NAITABAL LANGUAGE:	Language used by Naitabals to confuse enemies and adults.
NAITABAL LETTER:	A letter with a secret message That only Naitabals can read.
NAITABAL WHISTLE:	A piercing blast that deafens all adults within a hundred-metre radius.

David Schutte was born in Crouch End, North London. Brain surgeon, pop singer and Olympic athlete are just some of the things he never achieved. Apart from being an author, he is also a specialist children's bookseller. He lives in Hampshire with his wife and children.

DAVID SCHUTTE

WAKE UP, IT'S MIDNIGHT!

A Naitabal Mystery

To George

David Schutte

Junior Genius

First published in 1994
by Pan Macmillan Children's Books

Reprinted in 1996
by Macmillan Children's Books
Reprinted in 1997
This edition published in 2001 by Junior Genius
93 Milford Hill, Salisbury, Wiltshire SP1 2QL

ISBN 1-904028-01-2

1 3 5 7 9 8 6 4 2

A CIP catalogue record for this book
is available from the British Library

Printed in the U.K. by
Polestar AUP Aberdeen Ltd

TO

my mother and father

WITH LOVE

Rules for Speaking Naitabal Language

Words beginning with A: Add 'ang' to the end.
e.g. apple = *apple-ang*. The word 'a', however, is just *ang*.

Words beginning with B,C or D: move the first letter to the end of the word, then add 'ang' to the end.
e.g. banana = *anana-bang*; catapult = *atapult-cang*;
    disaster = *isaster-dang*.

Words beginning with E: Add 'eng' to the end.
e.g. elephant = *elephant-eng*.

Words beginning with F,G or H: move the first letter to the end of the word, then add 'eng' to the end.
e.g. fool = *ool-feng*; groan = *roan-geng*; help = *elp-heng*.

Words beginning with I: Add 'ing' to the end.
e.g. ink = *ink-ing*. The word 'I', however, is just *Ing*.

Words beginning with J,K,L,M, or N: move the first letter to the end of the word, then add 'ing' to the end.
e.g. jump = *ump-jing*; kill = *ill-king*; laugh = *augh-ling*;
    measles = *easles-ming*; night = *ight-ning*.

Words beginning with O: Add 'ong' to the end.
e.g. orange = *orange-ong*.

Words beginning with P,Q,R,S, or T: move the first letter to the end of the word, then add 'ong' to the end.

e.g. parrot = *arrot-pong*; queen = *een-quong* (notice that 'qu' stays together); rabbit = *abbit-rong*;
sausage = *ausage-song*; tickle = *ickle-tong*.

Words beginning with U: Add 'ung' to the end.

e.g. under = *under-ung*.

Words beginning with V,W,X,Y or Z: Move the first letter to the end of the word, then add 'ung' to the end.

e.g. vest = *est-vung*; witch = *itch-wung*; xylophone = *ylophone-xung*; young = *oung-yung*; zebra = *ebra-zung*.

For words beginning with CH,GH,PH,RH,SH,TH, or WH, move the 'H' with the first letter, but follow the 'first letter' rules.

e.g. chop = *op-chang*; ghost = *ost-gheng*; photo = *oto-phong*; rhesus = *esus-rhong*; shop = *op-shong*;
thistle = *istle-thong*; why = *y-whung*.

For plurals, keep the 's' in the original position.

e.g. book = *ook-bang*; books = *ooks-bang*;
pig = *ig-pong*; pigs = *igs-pong*.

MAP OF NAITABAL TERRITORY

Contents

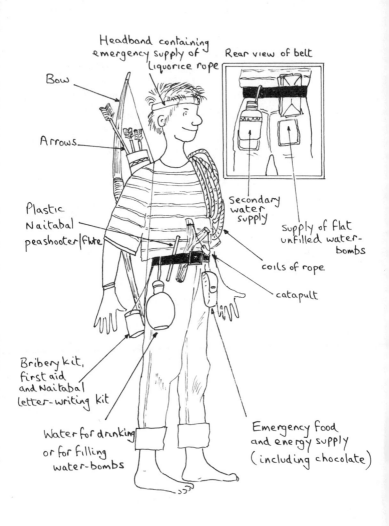

Headband containing emergency supply of Liquorice rope

Bow

Arrows

Rear view of belt

Plastic Naitabal peashooter/flute

Secondary water supply

Supply of flat unfilled water-bombs

coils of rope

catapult

Bribery kit, first aid and Naitabal letter-writing kit

Water for drinking or for filling water-bombs

Emergency food and energy supply (including chocolate)

Toby in Naitabal Battledress

CHAPTER ONE

The Mysterious Motionless Mr Maynard

"He's been like that for two days," said Ben. He was propped in one corner of the Naitabal tree-house, fanning himself with a wooden slat.

Charlotte turned to look at Ben.

"He can't have been," she said.

Jayne turned as well.

"Not for two *days*?"

Ben shrugged.

"Well, he has."

"Not all day..." said Charlotte.

"...And all night..." said Jayne.

"Probably not all night. But every time *I've* looked, he's been there."

Jayne and Charlotte were at the south window, taking it in turns to look through the telescope, which was mounted on a tripod, and aimed in the direction of Slug Island – known to ordinary people as Mr Maynard's garden.

"But he hasn't moved an inch in hours."

"He's like a sitting statue."

"I bet there aren't any pigeons on him," mumbled Toby through a mouthful of bark. He was sprawled face down on the branch that rose diagonally through the middle of the tree-house, breathing noisily. He rarely came to life much before noon.

The only Naitabal missing was Boff, who had been staying with his aunt for a few days' holiday. He was due back later that afternoon.

The motionless person under discussion was Mr Maynard, known to the Naitabals as HMS *Slugface*. He was a nasty, bad-tempered neighbour who had recently inherited the title of Naitabal Enemy Number One. "HMS" really stood for "Her Majesty's Ship" because he sailed around Naitabal islands, but now it also meant "Heartless, Mean and Selfish".

The incident happened when Ben had made the mistake of trying to cross the enemy's garden to get to Jungle Island. (It was Mrs Vormann's garden, really, but all gardens were seas or islands to the Naitabals.) HMS *Slugface* had seen Ben coming and had pounced on him from behind a tree. He had held him by the ears, pushed his shiny face next to Ben's, and told him with eyes bulging and lips snarling that he was a nasty little boy who ought to be boiled alive in golden syrup, stuffed with minced slug meat, and fed to the gulls.

"You're a nasty little boy, that's what you are! What are you?"

"Ouch! You're hurting my ears!"

"*What are you?*"

"Ow! A nasty little boy."

"And how should you be cooked?"

"Boiled in golden syrup."

"Boiled *alive* in golden syrup! And stuffed with?"

"Let go! Ow! Minced slug meat."

"And fed to the what?"

"Please let go, I won't trespass in your..."

"*And fed to the what?*"

"The gulls, the gulls!"

Then Mr Maynard had cackled like a mentally deranged mockingbird, manhandled Ben high into the air and dropped him back over the fence into his own garden.

Ben had crept back to the Naitabal hut, bruised in spirit. He had pronounced HMS *Slugface* completely mad, and warned that anyone crossing Slug Island had better take a suit of armour.

Through the telescope, the girls had been watching

Naitabal Enemy Number One at his study window. He was hunched over his desk holding a pen, his bald head glinting like a ping-pong ball, and bushy eyebrows drawn together in a deep frown. He was staring into his garden, and he hadn't moved from one hour to the next.

"It's difficult to see him properly," Charlotte complained, squinting through the eye-piece. "The Naitabal oak keeps waving its branches across, and when there *is* a gap, there are too many other trees in the way."

The Naitabals were trying to find a safe route to Jungle Island further to the south, but it meant crossing Slug Island to get to it. Jungle Island was the biggest unexplored tract in the whole of Naitabal territory. It had been unoccupied ever since Mrs Vormann had died at the grand old age of ninety-two, and the Naitabals were eager to explore it before it was sold.

"We can't get there without crossing Slug Island," Ben complained. "And with HMS *Slugface* glued at his window all the time, it's impossible."

The others nodded, except Toby, who had nodded off instead.

"I wish he'd move," said Charlotte.

"Who? Toby?"

"No! Mr Maynard. Toby won't move until lunch time."

"He's a writer," said Ben. "Writers don't move much."

"That's what Toby'll be, then. A writer."

"Perhaps he's dead," suggested Jayne cheerfully.

"Who, Toby?"

"Don't start that again!"

"*Mr Maynard*," said Charlotte, making it perfectly clear who she was talking about, "has written forty-nine books."

"Yes," said Jayne. "But my mum says none of them have been published."

It was a warm, sticky morning, and they had opened the north window of the tree-house as well as the trap-door in the roof. Above them, the huge canopy of the Naitabal oak swayed in the breeze. It shaded them from the direct rays of the sun, but they were still far too hot. Every now and then they drank fizzy drinks and fanned themselves with bits of fence that had blown off Cedric Morgan's ramshackle tree-house during the night.

"I always knew the Igmopong tree-house would come in useful one day," murmured Ben as he cooled himself with his strip of wood.

For once there was no danger of their conversation being overheard by the enemy Igmopong. Cedric Morgan and his gang were in Cedric's blow-up rubber boat on the lawn on Pigmo Island. Three of them were sitting in it in their swimming costumes, pretending to battle against a raging torrent of foaming rapids. The fourth, Andy, was throwing cups of water over them to add realism.

"It's pathetic!" said Charlotte, watching them.

"They really believe they're on a wild river," said Jayne. "You can see by the looks on their faces."

"And they're only doing it on Cedric's lawn because they're all frightened to go on the real river," said Ben in disgust.

Charlotte shook her head sadly as she swivelled the telescope towards Jungle Island and Mrs Vormann's house.

"I wonder if the people who buy it will be retired?" she said.

"They won't be able to run fast enough to catch us if they are," mumbled Toby. He said it without moving his mouth, which was still pressed against the branch in slumber.

The others grinned.

"People retire earlier these days," Charlotte warned him. "They're not all decrepit old miseries."

"And they get repaired," agreed Toby, ventriloquising. "All the bits that used to fall off get sewn back on again."

"Or replaced," said Charlotte.

14

"And just when you think you've got away," said Ben, "they switch on their batteries and run even faster."

"Well, I don't care who moves in," said Jayne, getting impatient. "I want to explore it while it's still empty."

"It's not empty," said Charlotte. "It's still got all Mrs Vormann's furniture in it."

"You know what I mean."

"That's why Mr Elliott's worried about burglars," said Ben.

"Why?"

"Because of all the furniture. That's why he asked us to keep a look-out."

"Well, we should be watching it at night, then," said Charlotte. "And it'd be much easier to watch it at night if we were there in the jungle."

Mrs Vormann's garden had been notoriously unlooked-after. Its overgrown trees and hedges had become a local landmark for aeroplanes.

Ben picked up a drawing he'd been working on.

"I wish Boff was back. He'd have this figured out in no time."

"Have what figured out?" said Charlotte.

"How to get there, of course."

Jayne and Charlotte abandoned the telescope and studied Ben's drawing to see if they could help.

"Why can't we just walk round by the road?" Jayne suggested as an afterthought. "That'd save us crossing Slug Island."

"Because we'd be seen, for one thing," said Ben. "And because it's an island, for another." He was shocked by Jayne's temporary lapse of Naitabal thinking. "We've got to get there without touching the ground."

"Why?" said Jayne.

"Well, if you touch the ground getting to an island, it can't be an island, can it? Islands are separated by water."

15

Jayne, who had only been a Naitabal for a short while, still had a lot to learn.

"Oh, I see – I think."

"But trees and fences don't count," said Charlotte helpfully. "We can use those to get there."

Another problem was getting past Pigmo Island. Ben, who usually volunteered for dangerous missions, had tried walking on top of the brick wall to get past them. He had been pelted with acorns and mud pies, and pushed off into his other neighbour's garden with a clothes prop. The neighbour, Miss Coates, had had words with him.

"I know we're friends now, Ben," she had begun, "but one of the beauties of friendship is that we do not fall into each other's gardens, isn't it?"

Ben agreed that it was. He conjured up a vision of Miss Coates walking on the wall and falling off into *his* garden. He had a fleeting image of her flying through the air, dress torn, white hair blowing like dandelion seed, and wrinkled knees dirty from climbing trees. It wasn't a pretty thought.

"So although we share some little secrets together," he heard her saying, "it doesn't mean that we have *carte blanche* to fall into each other's gardens, does it?"

Ben examined his T-shirt.

"It's not blancmange," he said. "It's a mud pie. Doris Morgan threw it."

"Not *blancmange*..." began Miss Coates, closing her eyes in pain. Then she decided not to bother, opened them again, and sighed. "Just try to stay out of my garden, Ben, there's a good boy."

"Yes, Miss Coates."

Ben brought his thoughts back to the problem of getting to Jungle Island.

"Even if we get past the Igmopong, the fence between Ben Tuffin Island and Charlotte Island is tricky because it's covered in that climbing stuff your mum likes."

16

"Honeysuckle," said Charlotte.

"I didn't know you cared." Toby's voice rose sleepily from the branch, and the visible part of his cheek creased into a smile.

"Shut up," said Charlotte. "And go back to sleep."

"And once we're past Charlotte Island," Ben went on, "we're on to Slug Island. We don't know what the terrain's like after that."

"Probably an express terrain," said Charlotte.

The others groaned, including Toby.

"Why don't we just go to Charlotte's and have a look from there?" said Jayne, mystified.

"Because it's cheating," said Ben. "We've got to get from the Naitabal oak to Jungle Island without touching the ground—"

"Seas..." corrected Toby.

"Sorry – seas. And we've got to recon-whatever-it-is first."

"Reconnoitre," said Toby.

"I do believe that boy's waking up," murmured Charlotte.

"Apart from that," Ben went on, "it's more fun."

"It would help if we could see better from here," said Jayne.

Toby rolled sideways off the branch and landed in a heap next to the others.

Charlotte studied him closely.

"So there *is* life after sleep..." she murmured.

Ben and Jayne grinned, and Toby yawned.

"If we want to see better," he said, logically, "we need a crow's nest, don't we?"

Three mouths opened wide in surprise as Toby's opened wider in another cavernous yawn.

"Toby's just been brilliant!"

Suddenly there was excitement in the air. None of them had ever succeeded in climbing the huge Naitabal oak any

17

higher than the roof of the tree-house. It would be a challenge to see how far they could get.

"Without breaking our necks," said Charlotte.

"Or our limbs," said Ben.

"Or the tree," said Jayne.

Toby climbed back on to the diagonal branch, and from there it was a simple pull up through the trap-door. Two minutes later they were all sitting on the roof of the Naitabal hut. They gazed at the majestic limbs that rose above them, fanning outwards in all directions.

"It looks difficult," said Jayne, frowning.

"It looks impossible," said Toby.

They continued to stare into the canopy for inspiration.

"We could bang spikes in and walk up them like a spiral staircase," suggested Ben.

"It might hurt the tree," said Charlotte. "And Naitabals don't hurt trees."

"We could sling a rope round one of those forks near the top and haul up a rope ladder," said Jayne.

"That's a good idea," said Ben. "Let's try that."

But before they had time to do anything, Toby pointed towards Slug Island and said, "Look!"

The others turned and looked.

"What?" they said together.

Cedric Morgan had heard Toby's exclamation as well, and hastily abandoned his team on the rapids. He bent himself double, thinking they couldn't see him, and rushed towards the fence to listen in to their conversation. Toby switched to Naitabal Language.

"*Aitabal-ning ruit-feng*," he said, still pointing.

It was gibberish to Cedric, but the other Naitabals followed the line of Toby's finger towards Slug Island and realised what he had said: "Naitabal fruit."

"*Aitabals-ning ungry-heng*," Toby added. "*Aitabals-ning et-geng ruit-feng.*"

18

Cedric Morgan still couldn't understand a word of the conversation. He crept back to his boat in disgust.

But the Naitabals were staring at what had been revealed through a gap in the leaves. On Slug Island was a small, but very full, pear tree, its branches heavy with plump, juicy fruit.

Jayne, Charlotte and Ben had translated Toby's Naitabal words. "Naitabals hungry," he had said. "Naitabals get fruit." They agreed in whispers that Naitabals were indeed hungry, and that Naitabals would like to get fruit. They descended into the hut again, the crow's nest temporarily forgotten.

"Let's just do it," said Ben, the adventurous. "If HMS *Slugface* doesn't move when he sees us, that'll prove that he's dead."

"Perhaps he's been turned into stone by an evil curse," said Jayne.

"Or a pillar of salt," suggested Charlotte, "like Lot's wife."

"Let's make it a race!" said Ben. "To Slug Island and back."

"That's not difficult," said Charlotte.

"It is. We're still not allowed to touch the ground."

"Seas," corrected Toby again.

"Sorry."

"Yes, that would make it a bit more tricky," agreed Charlotte.

"We'll take it in turns, and time each other."

"My watch shows the seconds," Jayne volunteered. "We can use that."

Ben's enthusiasm mounted.

"You have to start from inside the Naitabal hut. You're not allowed to touch the ground – sorry, the sea – until you get to Slug Island. Then you have to scrump a pear off his precious pear tree – to prove you've been there – and get back quicker than anyone else."

"And we've got to pick a pear off the *tree*," Charlotte said firmly. "No cheating and finding one on the ground."

Everyone agreed on the rules. It was just a matter of who went first.

"Going first is the most treacherous," said Ben. "The one who goes first has to blaze the trail and see if it makes old *Slugface* move."

"I'd rather go first than last any day," said Toby. "By the time the fourth one goes, HMS *Slugface*'ll be waiting."

"I'll go last, then," said Ben, who liked danger. "We should let the girls go first."

"We're just as good as you any day!" said Charlotte, flaring up.

"Yes!" said Jayne. "Better, most days!"

"We'll soon see, won't we?" said Ben. "How about Toby first, then Jayne, then Charlotte, then me?"

No one had any further objections, so Jayne took off her watch and laid it on the small table in the middle of the tree-house as Toby prepared to go. When Jayne said "Now!" he leapt on to the diagonal branch and was up and out through the roof in three seconds. He grabbed the hanging rope that was attached to the branch above Mr Elliott's chicken run, and hurtled downwards. He swung clean over the chickens, and his feet connected with the brick wall in the corner of Pigmo Island. He draped the rope across it, then balanced his way along the top and on to the fence that backed Ben Tuffin Island. The others watched as his untidy mop of wiry brown hair slowly receded into the distance. Now he was sitting astride the honeysuckle that covered Charlotte's fence, then he disappeared as he negotiated trees and shrubs. They checked carefully to make sure he didn't touch the ground.

Eventually, they used the telescope to track Toby's progress until he disappeared altogether. From the roof, Ben spotted a branch of the pear tree moving violently, followed

20

by the reappearance of Toby's head on a distant fence.

"HMS *Slugface* hasn't budged," said Ben.

"I told you he was dead," said Jayne, looking pleased with herself. Her bright blue eyes sparkled mischievously beneath her jet-black curls.

As Toby drew nearer on his return journey, they could see his jeans pocket bulging. At last he reached the rope, pulled on it with strong arms, and swung in mid air above the chickens as they fussed and clucked in the corner. He climbed the rope until he reached the branch, then heaved himself on to it, walked from there on to the roof again and dropped inside the Naitabal hut.

At the same moment, Jayne called out, "Four minutes and twenty-two seconds."

"He didn't even see me!" Toby laughed his silent laugh and collapsed on the floor, holding his pear aloft for all to see. Then he took an enormous bite out of it. "Naitabal fruit!" he added, through the mouthful. *"Aitabal-ning ruit-feng!"*

"Well done, Toby."

"Jayne next."

Jayne handed her watch to Charlotte. A few seconds later, Charlotte said, "Go!" and she went.

Ben's eye at the telescope watched Jayne until she reached the pear tree, then he swung it towards the distant study window. Could this be the same man, Ben wondered? The man who twisted children's ears if he caught them, and shook them until their teeth rattled? It was very strange, but true: the scourge of Naitabal territory, the terror of Slug Island, the motionless Mr Maynard still hadn't moved a muscle.

CHAPTER TWO

A Moving Chapter

Mr Maynard sat at his study window. His bulging eyes stared, unseeing, across his garden as the thoughts went round and round in his brain. They were the same thoughts that had been going round and round in his brain ever since Mrs Vormann, his next door neighbour, had died peacefully in her sleep in hospital at the grand old age of ninety-two.

Because there it was, all this time, sitting in her house. Probably no one else in the world knew of its existence. Only he knew it was there. He'd been a fool to leave it behind. If only he'd kept it until she came home... Looked after it for her...

But now it was too late. Or was it? Could he still get it? He didn't want anyone else to suspect that it existed, so laying his hands on it wouldn't be easy. He couldn't ask about it. He'd have to think of a way of getting it without raising any suspicions.

Perhaps he should break in and steal it – but then he might get caught – someone would see him, or they'd find his fingerprints... No. He could wear gloves and a disguise. But he might make a noise breaking the window... They'd catch him red-handed... Damn! He didn't want to spend the rest of his life in disgrace, finished as a writer. He hadn't had any inspiration for two weeks, so perhaps he was finished as a writer, anyway. That was why he wanted it.

But instead of doing something about it, he was just sitting there like a petrified log, day after day, staring into....

Vaguely, he was aware of someone in his garden. Normally, he would spring out of his seat, sprint across the lawn, grab the culprit by the ear, give him a good telling off, and throw him back where he came from.

But today he couldn't be bothered. He didn't have the energy. He didn't care if they chopped down his trees for firewood and made a camp in his rhubarb. Everything he wanted at the moment was to be found in Mrs Vormann's house. But how could he get it... without being caught?

His mind went round and round in the circle again, round and round.

He was half aware of another child – a girl. Then another girl. Then a boy. Each of them took one of his pears and ran off with it. He didn't care. He didn't need them. They could take them all.

His mind went round again, round and round...

It may have been an hour later that another disturbance seeped into his consciousness. He became aware of sounds coming from Mrs Vormann's house, next door. At last the circle was broken.

He moved.

Jayne did the return journey in four minutes and nineteen seconds, beating Toby's time by three seconds.

"I *know* he saw me!" Jayne panted, "because he *stared* right at me! But he still didn't move!"

Charlotte beat Jayne by ten seconds, but was disqualified for falling off a fence half way.

Ben failed to beat Jayne's official record, possibly because he wasn't satisfied with one pear, and stopped to fill his pockets even as HMS *Slugface* continued to stare at him.

Jayne was duly pronounced the winner. All in all, however, the mission to scrump Mr Maynard's pears had turned out to be less exciting than they'd hoped. Not one of them had come within a whisker of his or her life at the hands of the mad and dangerous monster of Slug Island. Neither had there been any hassle from the Igmopong, whose blow-up boat currently lay empty, and who had eventually emerged from Cedric's house with towels and drinks, long after the pear-tree raid had ended.

When the Naitabals were just finishing their second round of pears (compliments of Ben), Charlotte pointed through the west window.

"Look!" she said. "Mr Elliott's coming!"

The other Naitabals turned and looked. Sure enough, Mr Elliott was zig-zagging through the Sea of Debris towards them. It was his own garden, of course, but to the Naitabals it was the Sea of Debris. Mr Elliott was covered in dust as usual, and clouds of it flew off behind him, hanging in the air like the vapour trail from a jet plane. They could always tell which way Mr Elliott had come, just by looking for his dust cloud. Today there were kinks in it where he'd had to zig round the wheelbarrow, zag past the plastic drums and zig again to avoid the saw bench.

Four eager faces peered down at the upturned, dusty one of Mr Elliott.

"I'm going away for a couple o' weeks," he announced in a loud voice, "and I want you kids to keep an eye on the house."

Four mouths opened wide in amazement. Mr Elliott was a builder who worked seven days a week and never, never went anywhere. Mr Elliott going away was unheard-of.

"You'd better come up," said Ben, worried because the Igmopong had probably heard Mr Elliott's words. He could see their heads straining to listen for more, and Cedric Morgan was already starting to sidle towards the fence.

Charlotte opened the trap-door in the floor and carefully lowered the rope ladder. Mr Elliott's white figure swung on to it and climbed up with the ease of a monkey. Eight arms helped him inside. Charlotte and Jayne closed the trap-door, and a space was cleared for their guest to sit. Only three adults had ever been allowed inside the Naitabal hut. Mr

24

Elliott, who had built it for them, was the most important.

Ben went on watch at the south window, just in time to see Cedric Morgan, the leader of the Igmopong, creeping away.

"All clear," he said.

They were all excited about the prospect of looking after Mr Elliott's house, and waited anxiously to hear more details.

"Well," he began. He rubbed his forehead with his thumb and two fingers, and a baby cloud of dust rose in the air. "You know Mr Blake, don't you?"

The Naitabals nodded eagerly.

"And you know he called in to see me when he came down? Told me his troubles – and I know you kids were a great help sorting him out."

"He lives a long way away, doesn't he?" said Jayne.

"Couple o' hundred miles or more. He wants some work done on his house and I said I'd do it. It'll give me a break as well, see? Him and me can talk about the old days – we didn't get much chance before."

"When are you going?"

"In a few hours. But there's something else I want you to help me with before I go."

"We'll do it!"

"Anything!"

"Just name it!"

"It's Mrs Vormann's house—"

"Jungle Island," put in Ben.

"We haven't seen anything suspicious yet..."

"No. But you know she was a customer of mine for forty years," Mr Elliott went on, " – in fact, she was my very *first* customer – and she was always tellin' me she wanted me to look after her things when she died. Be her executor, like."

"I thought an executor was someone who chopped people's head's off," said Jayne, alarmed.

The others laughed.

25

"That's an executioner," said Toby.

"It means I have to sell her things and make sure everyone gets what she's left to them in her will," Mr Elliott explained. "That's why I asked you to keep an eye out, like. But now, see, I don't want to leave anything decent in her house while I'm away. I thought if we move the valuables to my house, you kids can keep an eye on 'em, same as my stuff."

The Naitabals had never been inside Mr Elliott's house, and they wondered if it was anything like his garden – full of rubbish. Ben turned to the others.

"We'll do it, won't we?"

"You bet!"

Charlotte's eyes were bright with excitement.

"Mr Elliott – ?"

"What's that, m'dear?"

"Is it – would it be – I mean..."

"Get it out, young lady, get it out."

"Can we *sleep* in your house while you're away?"

Ben, Jayne and Toby looked at Charlotte with shocked expressions on their faces. Mr Elliott laughed.

"You can do what yer like," he said. "It don't make no difference to me. You just keep an eye on the stuff for me, that's all. I don't want that Morgan kid nosing around while I'm away, either."

Cedric Morgan was Mr Elliott's next door neighbour, and there was no love lost between them.

"Don't worry, he won't," said Toby.

"When do we start?" said Charlotte.

Mr Elliott stood up, his head nearly touching the roof beams of the Naitabal hut.

"What about now?" he said.

The trap-door was opened again. Willing hands unfurled the rope ladder and helped Mr Elliott on to it. With a final puff of dust, he landed on the ground below and marched

26

briskly away. The others scrambled down the ladder, except Toby, who locked the Naitabal hut from inside. He went out through the roof, padlocked it, then crossed the three-rope bridge to Boff Island. They met up again in the road.

"How did you ever think of asking about staying there, Charlotte?" said Ben, as they made their way through the Sea of Debris.

"Pure genius!" said Jayne.

"It'll be a desert island," said Charlotte. "We can be marooned on it."

"And we've got to survive on just coconuts," said Jayne.

"We'll send messages in bottles," said Ben.

"And get a parrot," said Charlotte.

"And all have a leg cut off," said Toby.

"Don't be stupid, Toby," said the others.

"Sorry, I got carried away."

"You'd have to be," said Jayne, "if you had a leg cut off."

"Ha, ha, very funny."

"By the way," said Ben, looking up and down the road, "Cedric Morgan heard what Mr Elliott said about us looking after the house. He was behind the fence, trying to listen as usual."

"And succeeding," said Jayne.

"He can't do anything," said Charlotte. "Let's face it, he wasn't even in the queue when brains were in the shops."

"I don't think he knew there was a shop," added Ben.

Then the front door to Mr Elliott's house slammed, and he came puffing towards them, car keys dangling.

"Hey!" Jayne hissed at Ben. "I thought you said Naitabals couldn't go by road?"

"We can if we've got a Naitabal *ship*," said Ben. He pointed at Mr Elliott's battered van.

Mr Elliott threw open the doors, and the four Naitabals piled in. They sensed the presence of Igmopong. Cedric Morgan and his sister Doris were lurking behind their hedge

27

next door, still in their swimming costumes, and Andy and Amanda Wilson were peering through the crack in the side door of Pigmo Island.

Mr Elliott's van was exactly like his garden – full of rubbish. The first thing they had to do was to pile out again and move it all from the van into the skip that blocked the entrance to the Sea of Debris.

"Shouldn't we put down some sheets or something?" suggested Jayne, when the van was swept clean. "Otherwise, Mrs Vormann's furniture's going to get very scratched and dusty."

Mr Elliott agreed that this was a good idea, and a few minutes later he emerged with an armful of dust sheets.

At last they were ready. Mr Elliott started the engine, which sounded like a tin of marbles. He did a jerky three-point turn in the Straits of Brunswick, then rattled north, turned to starboard at Spider Island into Avenue Canal, and turned south into the Meadowlane-ian Sea. They bounced past Toby Island, past the Dreadful Sea where Miss Coates lived, past Ben Tuffin Island and Slug Island next door, and grated to a halt outside Mrs Vormann's house.

Mr Elliott unlocked the front door, and the Naitabals followed him over the threshold. Inside, the house was dull. The curtains and carpets were mostly gloomy reds and browns, and the walls were hung with dark Victorian paper. A strong smell of damp and furniture polish hung in the air.

"We'll 'ave to move this, first," said Mr Elliott. He used his foot to indicate the large wooden chest that used up half the width of the hall. "It'll be easier to get everything else out, then."

With two Naitabals at one end and Mr Elliott at the other, the chest was manoeuvred carefully out of the house. The girls then volunteered to stay in the van to load the furniture as the others brought it out.

"That's good," whispered Jayne when Ben, Toby and Mr

28

Elliott had gone back for more. "That means we'll have plenty of time to look at things."

While they were waiting, they lifted the lid of the chest. It was half filled with old coats and hats – the sort that Mrs Vormann used to wear when she went shopping. Jayne tried on one of the hats, and it came down over her nose. Charlotte giggled and tried on a different one. Soon they heard the removal party emerging from the house, and quickly put the things back and closed the lid.

As Charlotte turned away from the trunk, she suddenly caught her breath and stared up at Mr Maynard's house. Jayne followed her eyes.

There, standing at the upstairs window of the house on Slug Island, was HMS *Slugface* himself. He still wasn't moving, but this time his gaze and his frown were directed straight into the back of the van.

CHAPTER THREE

Naitabal Desk

One by one, the antique pieces of furniture came out – a small chest of drawers, a corner cupboard, a bureau, several carved chairs, and two inlaid tables that shone like glass. Jayne and Charlotte placed everything carefully in the van, using ropes and pads to keep things from falling over, and to make sure they couldn't rub together if the van went round a corner too fast.

Then a beautiful oak desk was brought out, and Jayne and Charlotte both fell in love with it at first sight. Its drawers were still in the house awaiting collection, but even without them, the desk was wonderful.

"It's a Naitabal desk!" breathed Charlotte. "Look at the carvings!"

Jayne's eyes were already poring over them. The whole of the front was hand-carved from solid oak, with oak leaves and acorns as the motif. They stood out like real leaves and real acorns on a real tree. There was a separate piece with more drawers that fitted on the top with pegs, which they lifted lovingly into place. It had an ornate rail round the back to stop things falling off, and all the wood was a medium brown. It shone as if it had been carved only the day before, but the girls knew it must be very old.

Jayne was kneeling, feeling the chunky carvings.

"That's funny," she said, suddenly. She stared into the empty holes that were waiting for the drawers to come and fill them.

"What?"

"This middle drawer, look!" She pointed into the hole

where the middle drawer belonged. "It ends at the back where the panel is, but the whole desk is much deeper than that. That means it's been blocked off!"

Charlotte stooped beside her and looked into the void. They took it in turns to crawl into the knee space and look up, to see if they could see any clue that might explain it.

"There's a hole you can put your finger in, but it doesn't do anything," said Jayne.

"It's just the way it's made," shrugged Charlotte. "If the drawer went in all the way, it would be far too long. They'd have to block it off. The hole's just to let air in, that's all."

Jayne wasn't satisfied. She reached her hand inside and pressed everywhere her fingers could reach. Nothing happened. Then she tried pushing her arm into the drawer spaces on either side of the middle one.

Hidden from sight, but visible to her probing fingers, she found a short peg, like a fat button. She pushed it and pulled it, but it didn't move. She reached into the opposite side to see if there was a peg there as well. There wasn't. Her fingers found the original one and pushed it and pulled it again.

"What are you doing exactly?" said Charlotte at last, when she had witnessed Jayne's normally pale face getting redder and redder in the hot van.

"There's something here," was all Jayne would say.

"What sort of something?"

Just then Ben and Toby arrived with a stack of drawers, so Jayne stood up, making signs to Charlotte not to say anything.

"They're all numbered, look," said Ben. He put them down and pointed to the roman numerals that were carved on the top of each drawer at the back. There were corresponding numbers at the entrance to each drawer space. "We're making some drinks," he added, as they retreated to the house. "So you can come in when you've done those."

"Look at the handles!" squeaked Charlotte. She held up one of the drawers. The front was carved from a solid piece of oak five centimetres thick. "The handles are big oak leaves, and you put your fingers behind them to open the drawer! Look!" She slid one drawer into place, then fondled the thick carved leaf with her fingers before pulling it out again.

Jayne made interested noises, but was soon back on her knees with one arm buried in the drawer space where she had found the peg. She pressed it and pulled it for the third time as hard as she could, but still with no result. Then she had a brainwave, and tried twisting it.

To her great surprise, there was a hollow "clonk", like an arrow thudding into a tree. Her eyes widened, and Charlotte said, "What was that?"

"I think I've found something." Jayne took her hand out and reached to the back of the middle drawer space again. "It's moving!" she said.

Instinctively, Charlotte looked out of the back of the van and along the road, to make sure that no one was watching what they were doing.

"What do you mean? What's moving?"

"This panel at the back." Jayne gave it a strong push, and there was a click. "Now I can't move it any more."

Frowning, she reached for the peg again with her right hand and twisted it, keeping her other hand inside the middle drawer space. There was the same resounding "clonk", but this time she felt the panel spring two centimetres towards her left hand.

Charlotte was kneeling beside her now, anxious to know what she had found. Jayne felt all round the loosened panel, but still couldn't get a grip to pull it out. Then she remembered the finger hole underneath, where people's knees went.

"I know!"

She dived down once more, pushed her finger into the hole and fiddled while her other hand pulled at the loose panel. With a thrill of excitement, she felt it slide towards her along the runners.

It was a secret drawer.

Jayne's eyes glowed as she held it up proudly and showed it to Charlotte.

"Wow!"

Inside the drawer was a buff folder. It was quite new, and it contained a thick sheaf of papers – perhaps more than three hundred sheets. Each page was typed with double spacing.

At the top of the first page, it said:

```
            SPY QUEST
               by
        Hermine Vormann
```

and underneath that:

```
           Chapter One
        The Death Papers
```

"It's a manuscript!" said Charlotte.

It was typed on an old-fashioned typewriter, and all the 'o's, 'p's and little 'e's were filled with ink in their middles, as if the typewriter letters were blocked up.

Before either of them had a chance to say anything else, they heard a little metallic click behind them. They both turned to look, and Jayne stood up. They had completely forgotten about Mr Maynard! He had disappeared from the upstairs window, and was coming out of his gate next door, on to the road.

Jayne slapped the folder shut, pressed it flat into the secret drawer, and pushed it back on its runners until it clicked into place.

Naitabal Enemy Number One walked towards them, feet turned inwards, leaning forward as if he might fall over any second. His face had changed from its usual miserable grumpiness to one they had never seen before: Mr Maynard smiling. It wasn't a nice smile, but an evil, smarmy one. His waxy smooth skin was wrinkled up in big, tight folds, as if it had never smiled before. And two rows of yellowing teeth, all different sizes, stuck out at odd angles, looking as if they wanted to bite someone.

"Ah!" he said, and the girls could feel the slimy slugginess of his voice crawling over them. "Helping with removals?"

Charlotte wanted to say, "No, we're paragliding down Mount Fuji," but thought it would be rather rude. Instead, she said "Yes" meekly.

He had reached them by this time, and immediately his well-manicured, smooth hands were running over things in the van, touching them, feeling them.

"What a beautiful desk," he murmured, moving his fingers along its carved edges. "I've never seen one as lovely as this."

Jayne and Charlotte instinctively drew back. They didn't want him touching things, but they couldn't stop him. They were relieved when they saw Mr Elliott coming towards them down the path. He was carrying three more of the drawers, and the boys were close behind him, carrying two more each.

"Ah! Mr Elliott!" cried Mr Maynard gleefully. He spoke as if they were great friends who hadn't met for years.

All the Naitabals knew he was just being an obnoxious slug, and Mr Elliott wasn't fooled, either.

"What's the problem?" he said, without smiling.

"I saw the children helping to move Mrs Vormann's things out, and wondered if I could help, that's all?"

Mr Elliott looked at him suspiciously.

"There are a couple o' heavy things," he admitted. "A bit too big for the boys."

"Pleasure! Glad to help!" said Mr Maynard.

Mr Elliott set down the three drawers he had been holding, and Ben and Toby set theirs down as well. Mr Maynard's eyes bulged and wandered hungrily over the contents.

"I couldn't help noticing this beautiful desk," he said, rubbing it again with his hand. "I saw it being brought out, and I thought – I must have a closer look at that."

"There it is, mate. No harm in lookin'."

"Is it sold? Or are you putting everything into auction?"

"What's it to you?" said Mr Elliott, very blunt.

The Naitabals stood in silence, looking from one grown-up face to the other, listening eagerly to every word.

"I'm asking," said HMS *Slugface*, slightly offended, "because I'm seriously interested in buying it." He turned on the false smile again. "I'll offer you a good price."

"Go on, then," said Mr Elliott, unconcerned.

"Five hundred."

A smile from Mr Elliott this time, and a short laugh.

"Huh! You must be out of touch, mate."

"What, five hundred? That's a good price."

"It might be what you call a good price, but it ain't what I call a good price."

Mr Maynard's deep frown returned. He stared hard at the desk, then again at Mr Elliott.

"A thousand, then," and he added hastily, "but I think that's being generous."

The Naitabals' builder friend laughed again, louder this time.

"Start talking five thousand, mate," he said, "and we could be in business."

"Five thousand!" Mr Maynard's voice rose to a whine. "It's not worth five thousand! Two thousand, and that's the limit."

35

"Come on," said Mr Elliott to the Naitabals. "Let's have that drink. Then Mr Maynard can help me with them heavy things."

Mr Maynard started to follow, but stopped suddenly on the path, glancing down at his tidy clothes.

"I'll have to get changed first," he said. "I'll be back in a few minutes."

The girls watched him disappear into his house.

Ben and Toby had already reached Mrs Vormann's front door, with Mr Elliott close behind.

"Come on, you two, don't dilly-dally!"

Jayne was full of excitement about their discovery, and wondered how to tell the boys without Mr Elliott overhearing.

Charlotte seemed to read her mind.

"Don't tell Toby and Ben yet," she whispered. "Let's keep it a secret for a while."

Jayne grinned and nodded as they followed the others back into the house for their drink.

The four Naitabals lolled in Mrs Vormann's big Victorian chairs, sipping orange squash and eating biscuits while Mr Elliott's quick little footsteps busied around them, deciding on which things ought to be moved out.

"Look at the typewriter!" said Jayne. She was just going to add, "I bet it's the one Mrs Vormann used to type her manuscript on," but stopped herself in time. She and Charlotte exchanged glances.

"It's ancient!" said Charlotte.

It was on the floor where the desk had been. It was black and tall and heavy, and it had the word "Oliver" in fancy gold letters on its front. The keys were round with shiny metal rims, and it had a half-black half-red ribbon in it. Jayne found a piece of paper in the waste paper basket, put it in, then turned the big heavy black roller to wind the paper through. Then she typed slowly, and lovely old, big letters slapped on to the paper, "D●wn with th● Igm●p●ng".

Ben and Toby looked over to see what she had typed, but quickly lost interest. But Charlotte knew what Jayne was doing. The 'o's, 'p's and 'e's were filled in in their middles where dust and ink had accumulated in the keys and never been cleaned. It was exactly the same in the manuscript.

"Let's clean it!" said Charlotte, suddenly.

She rushed into the kitchen and found a piece of rag and a safety pin. Then she leaned over the keys, sticking the pin into the centre of the letters and removing the little black blocks of dust and ink, and wiping them on to the rag. Then she used the cloth to wipe the keys thoroughly. A few minutes later, Jayne typed, "Up with the Naitabals" and the letters came out bold and clear with no black middles.

Satisfied, they finished their drinks. By this time Mr Elliott had organised several small things to be taken out, and the girls took them to the van. There was no sign of HMS *Slugface*.

"I bet he doesn't come and help," said Charlotte. "He just said that because he wanted the desk."

They put the rest of the drawers back, and the desk looked even more magnificent than ever. A few minutes later, Mr Maynard emerged from his house. His face was stretched into an even more strenuous smile, and he was wearing old clothes.

"Ready for the heavy stuff, girls?" he said.

Jayne and Charlotte poked their tongues out at his rounded back as he disappeared into the house.

Soon, they heard grunts and footsteps coming slowly towards the van. It was Mr Elliott and Mr Maynard, struggling with a tall bookcase.

"How about a hundred?" Mr Maynard was saying, out of breath, and Mr Elliott was saying, "No chance, mate. I'm not sellin' anythin' yet."

The men set the bookcase down, and Ben and Toby appeared, struggling with big boxes of books.

"It's only an old typewriter," Mr Maynard protested. "And a hundred's an excellent price."

"Sorry."

"Do you mean to tell me that after all this help I'm giving you, you're not even going to sell me an old typewriter for a hundred pounds? You'd only get a tenner for it if you were lucky."

"I'm definitely not sellin' anythin' yet," said Mr Elliott again, even more firmly than before. "Help or no help."

Mr Maynard's forced smile slowly faded as the remaining heavy items were brought out, and his offer was raised in stages to a hundred and fifty, with corresponding refusals from Mr Elliott.

At last the van was loaded with everything that seemed valuable, and they prepared for the return journey.

"There isn't enough room in the van to take you as well, Mr Maynard."

The Naitabals rather hoped he wouldn't come at all, but he had inexplicably cheered up again, and said, "I'll walk round – it'll do me good," and set off along the Meadowlane-ian Sea without further argument.

Mrs Vormann's house had already been locked up, but Mr Elliott slipped out of the driver's seat and disappeared inside again. He came out carrying something heavy, wrapped in a blanket, which he put on the floor at the Naitabals' feet.

"What is it?" said Ben.

"It's that typewriter," said Mr Elliott. "If old Maynard wants it that badly, like the desk, it must be worth a fortune."

CHAPTER FOUR

Teaching Harry Naitabal Language

Back at Mr Elliott's house, they stacked all the furniture and boxes into his large front room, which had previously been cleared for the purpose. Mr Maynard was already there, and at every opportunity his hands slid over things, feeling them, and his bulging eyes nosed into drawers and boxes and packing cases.

They hadn't been back many minutes before Cedric Morgan appeared on the pavement, fully dressed.

"Can *I* help, Mr Elliott?"

"No, you can't. You can clear off."

Cedric looked offended, but hung around, taunting the Naitabals each time they passed.

"That looks too heavy for you, Ben Tuffin. Mind you don't *strain* yourself." And, "Oh, dear, Charlotte, your jeans are split at the back."

"That's nothing," Charlotte riposted, not bothering to check. "Your *head*'s split at the back."

Eventually, Cedric disappeared, but no one noticed where he had gone.

When the unloading was finished, Mr Maynard made a final (unsuccessful) offer of a hundred and fifty pounds for the typewriter, then returned home on foot, looking stormy.

As soon as he had gone, Mr Elliott brought the typewriter in from the front seat of his van, and set it up on the carved oak desk, where it belonged.

"Is the desk really worth five thousand pounds?" Charlotte asked.

Mr Elliott laughed.

"'Course not!" he said. "I just didn't want him to have it, same as the typewriter. I don't like 'im – do you?"

The Naitabals felt more than satisfied, and made their way towards the Naitabal hut to plan the rest of the day.

Before they had gone very far, Charlotte stopped.

"I'll catch you up," she called to the others, and started running back to her house. "I'm going to see if Boff's written yet."

The postman hadn't been. He was much later than usual, but Mrs Maddison had heard reports that his van had had a breakdown, but he was on his way.

In a moment of weakness, Charlotte decided to pass the time trying to teach Harry, her seven-year-old brother, Naitabal language.

"You've got to *promise*," she told him, wagging her finger, "really *promise* never to tell anyone else how to speak it. Because only Naitabals can speak it, and when Naitabals speak it, they don't want anyone else to understand what they're talking about."

"Yes," said Harry.

"Do you promise?"

"Yes."

"Just saying 'yes' isn't good enough. You've got to say you promise."

"You promise," said Harry promptly.

"No. You've got to say 'I promise'."

Harry gazed at her with large innocent eyes.

"Do you promise as well?"

Charlotte took a deep breath and let it out slowly and noisily. Harry had earned his title as an honorary sub-Naitabal after helping the Naitabals in a recent battle with the Igmopong. Charlotte felt it only fair that he should learn to speak Naitabal, but she was already wondering if it was a decision she would regret.

"Now," she began, trying to think of an object that would

appeal to Harry. "If you want to say 'book' in Naitabal language, you take off the first letter and say 'ook'."

There was a silence.

"Well, say it."

"Ook," said Harry, pointing.

Charlotte held his finger down, raised her eyes to heaven and said, "It's nothing to do with *looking*, Harry. Now – you put the first letter back on the end, and say 'ook-b'."

"Ook—" Harry repeated the first part nicely enough, then tilted his head back, blew out his cheeks, and let the consonant fly from his lips like a champagne cork: " — *B!*"

"You don't have to say it like that," Charlotte admonished, calmly. "That was silly. Just say it nicely."

"Ook-b," came the obedient reply.

"That's better. Now, you put 'ang' on the end, and say *ook-bang*."

Harry said "Ook" quietly, then snatched an enormous breath and said "*BANG!*" with the full power of his lungs before Charlotte could stop him.

"And now sensibly?" she said, checking that her ears still worked.

"*Ook-bang.*"

"Good!" Charlotte beamed at him. "That's very good. So if book is *ook-bang*, can you tell me what boat is?"

"*Boat-BANG*," said Harry, giggling.

"No. It's *oat-bang*. You say it."

"*Oat-bang.*"

"Good. What's bed?"

"*Ed-bang.*"

"Excellent! Good boy! Now listen. Dog is *og-dang*. What is dog?"

"*Og-dang.*"

"Now if the word starts with a, b, c, or d, you put 'ang' on the end. But if it starts with e, f, g or h you put 'eng' on the end. All right?"

41

"Yes."

"And if it starts with i, j, k, l, m or n you put 'ing' on the end. Understand?"

Harry nodded.

"If it starts with o, p, q, r, s or t you put 'ong' on the end, and if it starts with u, v, w, x, y or z you put 'ung' on the end. Got that?"

Harry nodded confidently.

"Yes."

Charlotte watched the confident nod and realised that it was the confident nod he always used when he didn't understand anything at all. She decided to test him.

"So what's fish?"

"*Fish-bang,*" said Harry, without a moment's hesitation.

Charlotte sucked in her breath and let it out in a long, patient sigh. Where Harry was concerned, she had had years of practice with long, patient sighs.

"No, Harry – it's *ish-feng.* You don't just put 'bang' on the end of everything."

"*Pond-bang,*" said Harry, pointing at Charlotte lagoon out of the bedroom window.

"No, you take the first letter off—"

"*Ond-bang.*"

"No, you take the first letter off, and put it back on the *end....*"

"*Ond-bang-pond,*" said Harry.

"No! It's *ond-pong.*"

"*Ond-pong.*"

"That's better. Here, I'll draw a chart to make it easier." Charlotte grabbed a pencil and wrote on a piece of paper:

Starting letter	*Ending*
a, b, c, d	ang
e, f, g, h	eng
i, j, k, l, m, n	ing

42

| o, p, q, r, s, t | ong |
| u, v, w, x, y, z | ung |

"What's jumper?"

Harry put on his intelligent look, which bore little resemblance to the struggling brain behind it.

"*Umper...*" he began.

Charlotte pointed to the chart.

"*Umper-jing!*"

"Yes! Good boy! How about water?"

"*Ater...*"

Charlotte put a finger on the ending for him.

"*Ater-wung!*"

"Good! House?"

"*House-bang,*" announced Harry, tiring.

Charlotte was just about to give vent to another long-suffering sigh when the letterbox downstairs clattered. She leapt down the stairs instead.

"It's the *post-bang-man!*" declared Harry, chasing after her.

Charlotte grabbed the letter off the top of the assorted pile of letters that had just landed.

"Is there one for me?"

Harry ran round her, trying to look as she swung this way and that to hide them from his view.

"Of course not. Why would *you* get a letter?"

Harry considered.

"You get 'em. Why shouldn't I?"

"Because you don't write to anyone or send off for anything, that's why," said Charlotte. "And you haven't got any friends," she added heartlessly.

"I *have*...." he protested, hurt.

She didn't touch the others, but shouted "*Po-ost!*" to the family in general and ran outside, leaving Harry to search through the remaining pile suspiciously.

43

"I bet there's one for me...." she heard him murmur, then she was gone.

With the letter waving in her hand, she ran out of the house, along the road, in past the sign that hung drunkenly on Mr Elliott's lilac tree saying "NAITABALS – KEEP OUT", and on down the winding path that led to the Naitabal oak.

She delved into her pocket, brought out an acorn and took careful aim. She hurled it at the bell that hung next to the trap-door underneath the tree-house. It missed. She brought out another acorn and tried again. This time there was a satisfying 'ping', and moments later the trap-door was opened and the rope ladder was lowered.

Once inside, she waved the envelope at the faces that surrounded her.

"It's from Boff!" she said. "It was posted *five days* ago, so it's really late coming!" Then, without wasting any more time, she tore open the envelope, and read aloud.

"'Weather wonderful. Best on earth. I could write endlessly on the advantages of this place. It could never be boring. In fact, it's the most brilliant, stupendous resort in the entire world. Even heaven is not a patch on this. Boff.'"

"Gosh! He's having a really good time, then," said Jayne.

Charlotte spread the letter on the floor where all of them could see it.

"No he's not!" she said at last, squinting at it.

"It's a *Naitabal* letter," said Ben. "He's having a *terrible* time."

"An *awful* time," said Toby.

"He's bored out of his *mind*," added Charlotte.

Jayne was mystified.

"What are you talking about?" she said, wrinkling her nose. "He says he's having a wonderful time, and it's the best place in the world."

"We know what the ordinary letter says," said Ben. "With a *Naitabal* letter, it's what the *envelope* says that matters."

44

Jayne picked up the torn-open envelope and looked at it closely, turning it over.

"What do you mean? There's nothing written on it except Charlotte's address."

The other Naitabals looked at each other.

"Oh, I forgot," said Charlotte. "Jayne doesn't know the stamp code."

"No wonder," said Toby.

"What's the stamp code?" said Jayne.

"Look at the stamps on the envelope," said Ben.

"I just did. There's loads of them. Four at two pence, one at three pence, and – that's probably why it took five days – why doesn't Boff just put *one* stamp on like everyone else?"

"Because that's the code, of course. Four twopenny stamps means leave out *four* words, and the threepenny stamp means read *backwards*."

"What?"

"Look." Charlotte took a pencil and lightly underlined every fifth word in the letter, starting from the end, but ignoring Boff's signature.

"'Weather wonderful. Best on *earth*. I could write endlessly *on* the advantages of this *place*. It could never be *boring*. In fact, it's the *most* brilliant, stupendous resort in *the* entire world. Even heaven *is* not a patch on *this*. Boff.'"

"Now read them," she said, when she had finished.

Jayne read them.

"'Earth on place boring most the is this.'"

"No!" said Charlotte. "*Threepenny stamp*! Backwards!"

"Oh!" She took in her breath sharply in surprise. "'This... is... the... most... boring... place... on... earth'!"

"There!" said Toby. "So don't believe everything you read in letters."

"And if we want it to be *really* secret, we write it in Naitabal language as well!" said Ben.

Jayne shook her head in amazement. She had only joined

the Naitabals a short while before. In that time she had learned a lot, but whenever she thought she knew all there was to know, something else cropped up.

"So how does the rest of the code work, then?" she asked.

Ben explained.

"The number of twopenny stamps tells us how many words to miss out, a threepenny stamp means read backwards, and a fourpenny stamp means read forwards, but we'd still read forwards if there wasn't one. A fivepenny stamp means it's urgent, and a sixpenny stamp means deadly-peril-help-immediately."

"We've never needed to use a sixpenny stamp yet," mumbled Toby, bitterly disappointed.

"I think," said Ben, changing the subject, "that if Mr Elliott's going to be a couple of hours getting ready for his holiday, we might as well start making the crow's nest."

Everyone agreed, and they decided that the first thing they needed was rope. The Sea of Debris was so full of rubbish that they could usually find anything they wanted if they searched long enough. Rope, however, was a frequent requirement, and they already had a small stockpile hidden beneath a pile of broken garden statues and glass-less window frames.

Charlotte set off to get string, and found some in the skip that half-filled Mr Elliott's front garden. She returned in time to see Toby dragging a suitable quantity of rope towards the Naitabal oak.

On top of the tree-house, Jayne lashed extra weight on to the point of a Naitabal arrow. She coiled Charlotte's string on the roof, then tied it to the shaft while Charlotte held the other end.

Jayne prepared to take the first shot. The arrow had to be fired almost straight up, so the safest place was to sit on the edge of the trap-door in the roof, facing the tree. She flexed the bow and took aim. The arrow zoomed straight up. Then it zoomed straight back down, and both she and Charlotte had to duck sideways to avoid being hit.

Next it was Ben's turn. He didn't fare any better. This time the arrow went over a much smaller branch, and they had to pull on the string to get it back.

Toby's aim looked good, but Ben was standing on the string, and the arrow only got half way before bouncing back again. Toby demanded another try, but missed altogether the second time.

Then it was Charlotte's turn. Charlotte was determined to get it right. She aimed as carefully as she could, then let go. The arrow soared sweetly over the thick branch they were aiming for and hung limply on its far side. Charlotte gently flicked the string, and the arrow dropped lower and lower until Toby could reach it.

Then Charlotte attached the rope to the string. Toby pulled the other end, and the rope snaked its way upwards, over the branch, and back down into his hands. Stage one was completed – they had a rope over the highest thick branch.

Then Ben had an idea, and went down to the Sea of Debris again. Underneath a large tarpaulin was a stack of all sorts of furniture, most of it damaged in some way, including several wooden kitchen chairs. With a cry of triumph he pulled one out and ran back to the others.

The Igmopong by now had reappeared, this time balanced precariously in their ailing tree-house, and were watching everything the Naitabals were doing.

"If we hoist this up with a rope ladder attached, we can *sit* in the crow's nest!" Ben said, pleased with himself.

They tied the back of the chair to the rope and hoisted it up the tree. It rose slowly, like a flag up a flag-pole. When it reached the high branch, the Naitabals watched it for a few seconds. It swayed to and fro in the breeze, four metres above their heads. They hadn't attached a rope ladder yet – they could lower it again to do that – but they slowly realised

47

that it didn't look as safe as it had been in their imaginations. Ben, who was usually the first to risk anything, was now the first to speak his thoughts.

"It doesn't look very... safe, does it?" he said.

The others quickly agreed. None of them fancied climbing up and sitting on a chair that was swaying wildly on the end of a single piece of rope.

"What about two ropes?" suggested Jayne.

"It's pointing forwards," said Charlotte. "We'd still slide off the seat."

"Come back, Boff," said Toby. "We need you."

Boff was the one who usually solved the Naitabals' technical problems, but he wasn't due back from the stay with his aunt until later that afternoon.

Moments later Charlotte said, "Look!" in a loud, excited voice, and pointed towards the Sea of Debris.

The others turned their heads, and the sight that met their eyes was most unexpected. A figure was weaving its way amongst the rubbish that spilled across the path. It was dressed in a black suit with a waistcoat and a watch and chain across its front, and on its head was a black bowler hat. Its quick little steps, however, were unmistakable.

"Mr Elliott!" said four voices together.

CHAPTER FIVE

Row's-cang Est-ning

Never had they seen Mr Elliott like this. There wasn't the slightest trace of dust on him anywhere, and his face – or what could be seen of it under the bowler hat – was scrubbed bright pink.

Mr Elliott glanced up at the mention of his name, and saw the four of them balanced on the tree-house roof. He looked beyond them and saw the chair swinging precariously in the breeze.

"What's that supposed to be?" he said, nodding to it.

"We were trying to make a crow's nest," said Ben sheepishly.

"Coo! You won't do it like that!" said Mr Elliott.

With that, he climbed the rope ladder and joined them on the roof, still with his suit and bowler hat on.

The Naitabals couldn't keep their eyes off this new, clean version of their friend.

"What you need..." Mr Elliott began, but the sentence was never finished. He took a metal tape measure from his pocket and said instead, "Bring the chair down for me."

Intrigued, Charlotte and Jayne lowered the chair. Mr Elliott untied it, then attached the freed rope to a branch at one side. He gripped the other end of the rope where it hung in mid-air, and started to climb it like a tough little monkey, straight up.

"Which way do you want to see?" he called from the top.

"That way," said Ben, pointing towards Jungle Island.

Mr Elliott gripped the rope with his feet and one hand, and used his other hand to measure the main trunk with the tape measure. He held it out in front of himself, closed one eye, and moved his head from side to side.

"That's about it," he said. Seconds later, he had shinned down the rope, and two minutes after that he was on the ground with the Naitabals. He took off his jacket and waistcoat, threw them on to a nearby pile of tractor tyres, then rolled up his shirt sleeves.

"Right," he said. He told them which bits of wood he wanted fetching, then started sawing them up with a vengeance.

It had been exactly the same when he'd built the tree-house for them. It had taken him a whole week, and he just ignored his customers and worked at it every day until it was finished. It was the same now. He was supposed to be handing over his keys and going away on his first holiday for forty years, but here he was building them a crow's nest.

Mr Elliott marked most of the pieces he wanted and set the Naitabals to work sawing them up. While they were doing it, he fetched two long ladders and lashed them together side by side to make them wider. He nailed big blocks to the roof of the Naitabal hut, and with the Naitabals' help, hauled the new ladder up, propped it against the rising branch, and secured it in place with ropes.

A lot of hammering and sawing later, wooden frames were hoisted up the tree, and by the end of two hours, the Naitabals had their crow's nest, safe and strong, with a wooden ladder leading to it from the roof of the Naitabal hut, securely fixed at both ends.

Mr Elliott grinned, showing National Health teeth.

"There you are, mates," he said. "A bit safer than yours."

"Thanks, Mr Elliott!"

"That's wonderful, Mr Elliott!"

"Mr Elliott, you'll be late!"

He was hot from all his work, especially in his black suit trousers and bowler hat, but he put his waistcoat back on, then his jacket, and handed the keys of his house to Charlotte.

"I'm off," he said. Then he bared his false teeth in another smile and walked away, satisfied.

The Naitabals went up to see him off in his van, and waved until he was out of sight. As soon as he had gone, they tumbled back through his front garden, past the overflowing yellow skip, and down the winding path to the tree-house. They gazed with pride at the crow's nest, too excited to decide who should be first to try it.

"It should be Toby," said Charlotte at last, generously. "He thought of it."

"Yes, it should," said Jayne.

"Yes," agreed Ben. "You go up first, Toby."

Toby beamed with pleasure. They all went up the rope ladder into the tree-house, up on the diagonal branch and on to the roof, where Toby grabbed the sides of the new ladder and climbed slowly upwards, one step at a time. At the top of the ladder he turned to look down, grinning.

"This is great," he said. He lifted the safety bar from the front of the solid chair that Mr Elliott had made, then twisted into the seat. He brought the bar back down to lock himself in place. "It's brilliant!"

The chair was supported by the ladder, by two wooden frames around the rising branch, and by safety ropes connected to the branches above.

"Safe as houses," said Toby. "And the view – wow!"

Soon, the other Naitabals were clamouring for a turn. One by one they climbed the wide wooden rungs, and one by one sat in the big chair.

"It's like a throne," said Charlotte, feeling the chunky arm-rests. "I can survey all Naitabal territory from here."

It was true. The crow's nest was higher than many of the houses, and she could see cars going along the Meadowlane-ian Sea past the Dreadful Sea to her left, and in the Straits of

51

Brunswick beyond Pigmo Island to her right. In front of her lay Ben Tuffin Island, with Charlotte Island to its right, and further away, Slug Island, Jungle Island and the other unexplored regions.

"It's a bit scary," said Jayne when it was her turn, but she soon got used to it, and was just as excited as the others.

"Any sign of the Igmopong?" said Ben.

"Nothing. They've disappeared."

"Good. They probably won't notice we've got a crow's nest for ages."

"They'll see the ladder."

"Yes, I forgot about that."

Jayne came down, and Ben went up. For a few glorious moments he was the captain of a pirate ship, cutlass in teeth, climbing the rigging to oust a deadly enemy above. He reached the top. He grappled with the villain, and threw him, all twenty stone of him, into the stormy sea below.

The Naitabals' next visitor was Harry. He was running through the Sea of Debris, springing over the multitude of obstacles. He turned once to glare at something that had nearly tripped him up, then bounded on, two pieces of paper flapping in his hand.

Charlotte opened the west window.

"What are you doing in Mr Elliott's garden, and what do you want?" she said sternly.

"Gotta letta," said Harry. Then, remembering, added, "Letter*bang*."

"It's not letterbang, it's *etter-ling*," corrected Charlotte. Then – suspiciously – "Where from?"

"Postmanbang."

Charlotte threw her eyes to heaven, but didn't bother to correct him this time.

"Let me see it."

She closed the window, and the rope ladder was lowered.

Harry rushed to it, hoping for a rare glimpse inside the Naitabal hut, but Charlotte was already on her way down and telling him to get off. He handed her the letter, but still had another one in his hand.

"There *was* one for me, see!" he said.

"It's another one from Boff!" said Charlotte, glancing at it. Then, to Harry: "You're not supposed to open other people's letters. It's very, very naughty."

"It said 'Naitabals' an' I'm an Onnermy Sub-one, so I could."

"No, you couldn't!" Charlotte looked cross. "Letters to Naitabals can only be opened by chief Naitabals, and you're not a chief Naitabal. And where's the envelope?"

Harry turned slowly and raised a small, bent finger towards the skip.

"Skipbang," he said.

Charlotte groaned. It was legendary that anything that went into the skip was as good as lost for ever. Ben had suggested that Mr Elliott's skip was really a black hole, as yet undiscovered by science.

"You might as well go, then. And don't you *ever* do it again. You can bring us letters, but don't open them in future. All right?"

Harry nodded.

"And what's that in your other hand?"

"Nuvver letta," said Harry. "Twobang."

"Let me see it."

Harry handed it over, and Charlotte scrutinised the typed envelope. At least he hadn't opened this one.

"It's for Mr Maynard!" she screeched. "Where did you get it?"

"It was wiv ours!" came the over-loud reply. "I gotta deliver it! Mum said."

Charlotte handed it back to him.

"Well, make sure you do. It might be important. Do you

know how to get to his house?"

Harry gave his confident nod, and Charlotte groaned.

"That means you don't know, doesn't it? Well, it's the one next to Ben's. Not Miss Coates's. The other side. Off you go, then."

"Byebang!"

Harry bounced away, almost tripping over the same object again, and turned once more to glare at it malevolently. Charlotte held the Naitabals' letter in her teeth and climbed back up the rope ladder.

"I tried to teach Harry Naitabal language," she said, shaking her head sadly as it appeared inside the trap-door. "He thinks you just put 'bang' on the end of everything!"

The others laughed as they waited for Charlotte to unfold the letter. It said:

Naitabals!

Greetings from my desk to everyone in the Naitabal oak. Tried to get you on the telephone, but you're hardly ever in. I really must apologise, but it's nearly three days since I wrote. It was sad about Mrs Vormann, wasn't it? My aunt says that she was ninety-two.

I must book a seat on the train. The problem coming was I couldn't find one. Looking forward to seeing you. Warm the tree-house if you can.

Boff.

"It reads just like an ordinary letter," said Jayne. "I wonder if it's really a Naitabal one?"

"It probably is," said Toby. "Knowing Boff, he'd want to make it a Naitabal one, even if he didn't have anything much to say."

"Without the envelope, we can't tell, easily," said Charlotte. "We'll have to try different combinations and see

54

if it makes sense."

"I'll try backwards," said Jayne. "I'll miss out four words, the same as last time." She translated slowly.

"'Can... warm... looking... was... the... must... that.... wasn't.... was.... days.... apologise.... ever.... the.... tried.... everyone.... greetings.'!"

"Doesn't make much sense," said Toby. "I've got a better one – listen." He read backwards quickly, skipping three words each time. "'Can the to find coming the book? Was aunt Vormann was, since it's really. Hardly the to the desk Naitabals.'"

They all laughed.

"It sounds Welsh," said Ben, imitating: "'Can the to find coming the book?'"

"If you try missing out two," said Charlotte, "it begins 'Can tree-house you forward find, was the on book ninety-two...' Mmmm... I don't think it's that, either."

There were more grins, and then it was Ben's turn. He grabbed the letter and frowned, studying it closely.

"It's five!" he said suddenly. He grabbed a pencil and lightly underlined each word, starting at the end and missing out five words each time.

Naitabals!

Greetings from my *desk* to everyone in the Naitabal *oak*. Tried to get you on *the* telephone, but you're hardly ever *in*. I really must apologise, but *it's* nearly three days since I *wrote*. It was sad about Mrs *Vormann*, wasn't it? My aunt says *that* she was ninety-two.

I must *book* a seat on the train. *The* problem coming was I couldn't *find* one. Looking forward to seeing *you*. Warm the tree-house if you *can*.

Boff.

55

The others looked over his shoulder as he read the underlined words backwards, out loud.

"*Can you find the book that Vormann wrote? It's in the oak desk!*"

Jayne and Charlotte, shocked by the message, and thinking of their secret, exchanged hasty glances.

"It *is* a Naitabal letter!" said Jayne breathlessly, covering up. "Not an *ordinary* letter, after all!"

"I didn't know Mrs Vormann was a writer," put in Charlotte, all innocence.

"I wonder what sort of book it is?" said Ben. "I hope it's a mystery."

"Mr Elliott's gone," said Toby. "So there's nothing to stop us looking for it right now."

Jayne, half disappointed that the secret she shared with Charlotte would be given away so soon, said, "I wonder why Boff wants us to find it?"

"Perhaps his aunt told him to," said Charlotte. "She was born in Boff's house, wasn't she – like his dad? Don't you remember when she used to live there? I bet she knew Mrs Vormann for years and years, like most people round here."

"Perhaps it's a really important manuscript, and Boff's aunt's afraid of it being stolen from the empty house," said Ben. "Perhaps Mrs Vormann was really a double spy working for the KGB, and—"

"But Boff doesn't know the desk has been moved to Mr Elliott's house!" Jayne interrupted. She brightened at the thought of keeping their secret a little longer.

"That's right!" said Charlotte. "It's safe there. We can leave it until Boff gets home."

"We'll put three acorns on his doorstep, so he knows there's a meeting straight away!" said Ben. "Then we can plan everything properly."

After more discussion it was agreed that no one would go into Mr Elliott's house until Boff came back. Then he could

56

share the fun. This settled, they climbed on to the roof of the Naitabal hut and took it in turns to sit in the crow's nest with the telescope, surveying Naitabal territory.

"What's HMS *Slugface* doing?" said Ben, when Jayne was on look-out.

"I can't see what he's *doing*," said Jayne. "But he keeps throwing his bald head back and laughing like a maniac."

CHAPTER SIX

Allenge-chang

Cedric Morgan sat in his ramshackle tree-house, chin in hands, gazing over the fence towards the superior tree residence of the Naitabals. Its superiority was so startling that it was physically painful for Cedric to think of it. But it was only better, of course, because Mr Elliott had built it for them.

"I bet if *they* had to build one themselves, it wouldn't be half as good as ours," he muttered, turning to the three members of his gang, who were with him.

"Half as *what* as ours?" said Doris, his belligerent red-headed sister, coming forward. "Did you say *good*?" She pulled a small piece of wood off the wall and tossed it over the side.

Andy and Amanda Wilson, the other two members of the gang, hovered in the background.

It was true that Cedric's gang had built their own. It was also true that its floor sloped dangerously, that its walls were falling apart (assisted by Doris and last night's visiting wind), and that its roof was only two doors tied together with string. It had long been Cedric's dearest wish to own the Naitabals' tree-house, even for just a few days. But whenever he tried to trick them out of it, his gang always seemed to finish up worse off.

If only he could think of a plan that would work...

"I wish I knew what they're up to," said Cedric.

"You said what they're up to already. You said Mr Elliott told them to look after his house while he's away."

"I know that. But they're up to something else. They've

come back with loads of furniture, and they've built that look-out thing—"

"Crow's nest," put in Amanda Wilson.

"Yeah," said her brother, Andy. "Iss a crow's nest."

"I just said that!"

"Yeah. So did I."

"Oh, shut up, you two!" said Doris.

"*They built that look-out thing,*" Cedric went on loudly, "and they keep going up in it and looking through a telescope an' shouting 'Land Ahoy!' and 'Yo ho ho and a can of Coke'."

"We'll have to spy on 'em better, then, won't we?" said Doris.

"I don't see how we can spy on 'em better when they're miles away up a tree," said Amanda.

"Nor can I," said Andy.

"I mean spy on them when they're in Mr Elliott's garden," said Doris irritably. "That's when they talk about what they're doing."

Cedric threw out his hands in a frustrated gesture.

"But whenever we go near the fence, they start talking a funny language," he said.

"It doesn't mean anything," spat Doris. "They just talk any old rubbish. And thickies like you think it's a language."

"It *does* mean something. Anyway – even if it doesn't, it'd be a good idea for *us* to have a language so that when they come near *our* fence we can start talking it."

"I see." His sister planted her feet apart and put hands on hips in an aggressive gesture. "So we just have a language, do we? Just suddenly?"

"Ye-es."

"Just a whole language, like French or German, that's taken about three thousand years to make up?"

"It'd be longer than that," put in Andy.

59

"How long, then, clever?"

"Four thousand, at least."

"Oh, shut up, Andy. Well?"

"No-o. Not like French or German. A sort of language that's easy to learn."

"Oh, I see." She goaded him. "Go, on, then. Make up a language. Go on. Start now."

Cedric was nonplussed.

"Go on," Doris pursued him. "Start with one word, that's all. What's the word for 'tree' in this wonderful language of yours? Just tell us that?"

"Yeah," said Amanda. "I bet you can't think of one."

"Yeah," said Andy.

Cedric stood looking at them. Somehow they had inched their way into a hostile group, huddled together on the sloping floor, facing him.

"Come on," taunted Doris. "What's your word for tree?"

Cedric's eyes ached as he returned her aggressive stare. The silence between them grew longer. Then, just as Doris was starting to say something about the size of his brain, and how well it would fit into a matchbox, and still leave plenty of room for matches, Cedric suddenly spluttered.

"*Eert*," he said.

"What d'you mean, *eert*?"

"*Eert*."

"That's your word for tree, is it? *Eert*?"

"Yeah."

Cedric felt proud of himself. He didn't know what had made him think of it. It was just "tree" backwards. But his silly old sister and the others hadn't even noticed.

"What's 'brother', then?" said Doris, suspiciously.

"*Rehtorb*," said Cedric, promptly. Making up a language was a lot easier than he had thought.

"What's 'television'?"

Cedric needed a few seconds longer for that one.

60

"*Noisi velet,*" he said.

Doris was secretly impressed, but continued to look at him sideways.

"You're just doing what the Naitabals do," she accused him. "Just making up any old rubbish."

"No I'm not," said Cedric. He stood confidently, his mind poised for the next word. He'd always been below average at reading, but turning words backwards seemed to come easily to him.

"What's 'pencil', then?" barked Doris.

"*Lisnep,*" said Cedric. (He couldn't spell "pencil" very well.)

His sister tested him with a few more words, but neither she nor the others could work out what Cedric was doing. As a result, his prestige (usually fairly low) rose slightly. He promised that he would teach them Cedric Language if they gave him the respect he deserved as leader.

"'Walk in the park'," snapped Doris, suddenly.

"*Klaw ni eht krap,*" said Cedric, and thus put himself firmly in charge again. "Now – what're we gonna do to get into their tree-house?"

"Challenge 'em," said Doris. She swivelled defiantly, now directing her venom towards the Naitabal hut. "Then we can find out its secrets, and build one of our own – even better."

"Challenge 'em to what?"

"Challenge 'em to something, and if they can't do it, we get their tree-house for a week."

"And what if they *can* do it?"

"They get ours for a week."

Cedric snorted.

"Don't be thick. They wouldn't want ours – except for firewood."

"What about our blow-up boat?"

"What about *my* blow-up boat?" said Cedric, moving on the defensive.

"If they can do the challenge, they can borrow our boat for a week, and if they can't, we get their tree-house."

"But I don't want 'em to have my boat for a week – it's the only thing I've got they haven't got. I saw them looking at us when we were playing in it just now. I think they were jealous."

Doris twisted her mouth sideways.

"Then we'll have to make sure it's a challenge *they can't win*, won't we?"

Cedric grinned a crafty grin.

"We could challenge 'em to a bike race."

"They'd win."

"A swimming race."

"They'd win."

"A cross-country race."

"They'd win."

Cedric grudgingly admitted that Doris was probably right. His gang were all rotten at the things he'd suggested, and the Naitabals would beat them silly. He wasn't even sure that Andy could ride a bike at all, and Amanda certainly couldn't swim.

"You suggest something, then, clever clogs," he said sarcastically. "You think of something we could beat 'em at."

Doris looked taken aback for a few moments, until a crafty smile slowly dawned across her face.

"Cheating," she said, triumphantly.

"What d'you mean, cheating?"

"What'd'ya think I mean, stupid? We *cheat* 'em. It doesn't matter what we *challenge* 'em to, as long as we can *cheat*."

Slowly, Cedric began to see the logic of his sister's argument.

"I see," he said, grudgingly. "It doesn't matter, does it?"

"If it was cycling we could let down their tyres..."

"Or take a link out of their chains..."

"Or slacken their brakes..."

"That'd be no good," said Doris. "They'd go faster."

"Oh, yeah."

"If it was cross-country running we could put thistles in their shoes..."

"Or change the signpost so they went the wrong way..."

"Or let a bull into the field just as they were going past..."

"That'd be no good," said Doris. "That'd make them go faster as well."

"Oh, yeah."

"If it was swimming, we could hook fishing lines to their costumes, and when they got nearly to the finish they wouldn't be able to go any further, and we'd catch 'em up and beat 'em."

"They'd swim right out of their costumes, just to win," said Doris. "They wouldn't care."

"We could wear flippers. We'd beat 'em easy with flippers..."

"I can't swim," said Amanda.

"I bet you could with flippers," said Andy. "And you could cheat by wearing armbands."

"If it was rowing, we could make a hole in their boat..."

"Or make holes in their oars..."

"Or tie an anchor underneath..."

"Yes," said Cedric, suddenly cross. "And if someone can tell me what it's going to *be*, and how we can cheat without Ben Tuffin and his lot *noticing*..."

They all frowned, deep in thought.

"Don't you see?" said Doris at last. "It doesn't matter what the challenge is, we'll just *cheat*! Let *them* choose!"

Back in the Naitabal hut, the subject of conversation was still HMS *Slugface*.

"But he *never* laughs!"

"He does when he's caught someone in his garden and threatens to cut them up into little pieces and feed them to the gulls."

"There's no one in the study with him, is there?"

"Not that I can see."

"For two weeks he's been miserable—"

" – As he usually is—"

" – And motionless—"

" – And now he's laughing his head off."

"It doesn't make sense."

Mr Maynard's strange maniacal laughter continued to be observed and discussed by the Naitabals until their thoughts were interrupted by a familiar cry.

"Igmopong!"

The word never made sense to ordinary people, but to the Naitabals it meant that Cedric Morgan had crept up to the fence and was trying to listen in to their conversation.

They dropped their voices.

"*Ere-whung?*"

"*Ehind-bang e-thong ence-feng,*" said Ben, clarifying the situation.

"He can't hear us if we whisper," said Charlotte.

They were back inside the hut, with the exception of Toby, who was on watch in the crow's nest. It was too hot to close the windows, so the others spoke as quietly as they could.

"I wonder what he wants?"

It didn't take too many seconds for them to find out. Cedric's round, pale face appeared briefly over the fence-top, accompanied by two chubby arms and a home-made bow and arrow. He pulled back the string. The arrow flew in a straight line (for once), hit the trunk of the Naitabal oak, and hung there, sagging precariously while the force of gravity tried to decide what to do with it.

Jayne tumbled down the ladder and rescued it before gravity had finished making up its mind.

"It's a message," she said, handing it to Ben, who was usually in charge when Boff wasn't there.

As Toby came down to join them, Ben removed the elastic band and opened the roll of paper that was wound round the shaft. The note was written in pencil, in capitals, and wasn't signed:

WE CHALLUNGE YOU TO ANYTHING YOU WANT.
IF WE WIN, WE SPEND A WEEK IN YOUR TREE-HOUSE.
IF YOU WIN, YOU BORROW MY BOAT FOR A WEEK.
COWARRDS NEED NOT APPLY.

Cedric had been proud of the last line. He had seen something similar at the end of a job advertisement, and had adapted it for his own purpose.

The Naitabals read it in turn.

"He can't spell 'challenge'," said Charlotte.

"Or 'cowards'," said Jayne.

"But we can't ignore it," said Ben. "He'd call us cowards for ever more if we did."

"But all we've got to do is challenge them to climbing a rope and they'd lose," said Toby.

"He must know that."

"There's a catch somewhere..."

They all thought for a few minutes.

"He knows we'll think of something that's fair," said Ben.

"You're right. He knows we wouldn't challenge them to running or swimming or something, because we'd win too easily. It wouldn't be any fun."

"Perhaps he's got brains after all," said Jayne.

"Natural cunning, more like," said Toby. "Some people are like that. As thick as a hippo sandwich, but dead crafty."

"What matters," said Ben, "is that Cedric and the Igmopong still want the Naitabal hut for a week."

"And we wouldn't mind their boat, either," said Toby.

65

"We could take it on the river," said Ben.

"And go miles upstream."

"And miles downstream."

"And under bridges."

"And down rapids."

Slowly, they came back to reality.

"Let's think of a challenge," said Charlotte.

There was a brief lull while they all exercised their brains.

"It's got to be something we're not better than them at," said Ben, summing up.

"That doesn't leave much," said Charlotte. "We're better than them at everything."

"But we've got to give them a *chance*."

"That's it!" said Toby. "Give them a chance! A card game – or monopoly – they'd have as much chance as we had."

"Not much fun, though. Not for a challenge."

"Rolling dice?"

"Too simple."

Another silence.

"I know!" said Ben.

"What?"

"A treasure hunt!"

"But one of us would know where the treasure was hidden," said Jayne, wrinkling her nose.

"No! *We'd* hide something, and *they'd* hide something, and the first one to find the other one's treasure is the winner!"

Toby was doubtful.

"They'd just hide it somewhere ridiculous."

The others had doubts, too.

"At the bottom of the river, for instance."

"Or he'd take it for a paddle in his blow-up boat and drop it overboard half a mile away."

"No," said Ben, still bright with his idea. "There'd be

rules. It'd have to be something big so it couldn't be buried. And we'd only have so much time to hide it, and—"

"Yes!" said Charlotte. "We could wait while they hid theirs, and then they could wait while we hid ours."

Suddenly they were all eager for the challenge. It began to sound exciting, and the rules came thick and fast.

Twenty minutes later, a Naitabal arrow thudded into the base of the beech tree that housed what was left of the Igmopong hut. It said:

CHALLENGE ACCEPTED
MEET US TOMORROW WHEN BOFF'S BACK
COWARDS CAN STAY IN BED

CHAPTER SEVEN

Py-song Est-quong

Soon after tea, a cry from Charlotte in the crow's nest brought Ben, Jayne and Toby jostling on to the roof of the Naitabal hut again. Her voice came down to them in an urgent whisper.

"There's someone in Mrs Vormann's house!"

Ben jumped on to the ladder and stood on the bottom rung.

"Can you see who it is?"

Charlotte was still squinting through the telescope, trying to identify the intruder.

"No – I think – yes! It's Mr Maynard – HMS *Slugface*!"

"Are you positive?" By now, Ben had climbed several more rungs towards the crow's nest, and was standing just below Charlotte's knees.

"Yes, it's definitely him. He's not at his study window – I checked. And I can see his bald head and his bulging eyes and shiny skin."

"Can I have a look?"

Ben swung sideways to let Charlotte pass so they could change places in the crow's nest. He had a long look through the telescope, and came to the same conclusion. It was definitely HMS *Slugface*. Then Toby stayed on watch while the others climbed back inside the Naitabal hut to discuss the situation. It was cooler now, and they could close the windows and the trap-door in the floor, and so have less chance of being overheard by the Igmopong.

"What shall we do?" Ben said, when the three were back inside. "Mr Elliott's gone, so we're sort of responsible for Mrs Vormann's house as well, aren't we?"

The others agreed that they sort of were.

"Did you notice when we were there how he kept touching everything and poking his big nose where it didn't belong?" said Jayne in disgust.

"Yes."

"I wonder what he's after?" said Ben.

"He wanted the desk badly," said Charlotte.

"And the typewriter," said Jayne.

"Yes – but what do we do about him snooping around in her house?" Ben repeated anxiously. "He might steal something."

Toby's voice floated down from above.

"It's too late," he said, as he abandoned the crow's nest and climbed down into the hut. "He's back in his study."

"It was definitely him," said Charlotte.

"Yes," said Ben. "Me and Toby saw him as well. It was definitely HMS *Slugface*."

Jayne had been getting more and more agitated, and said at last, with a glance towards Charlotte, "I do wish Boff would come back soon. Then we can look for that book Mrs Vormann wrote."

They didn't have long to wait. Only ten minutes later they heard the sound of an acorn hitting the under-side of the hut, then another, then another. None of the Naitabals moved. They all knew the rules. Soon, there was a gentle "ting" as an acorn hit the bell that hung beneath the floor, making it sing and dance. At last it was a valid Naitabal call, and they could get up and answer it.

Below them, as expected, the bespectacled Boff was waiting to be let in. Without wasting any time, they lowered the rope ladder for him, welcomed him back, then started to bring him up to date with Naitabal affairs. He listened to the first part in silence, but soon interrupted.

"You haven't got the book yet, then?" he said, anxiously.

"We only got your letter at lunch time," said Charlotte.

69

"As you were due back this afternoon, we thought we'd wait."

"We thought we could find it together," said Jayne.

"And there were slight complications," added Toby.

"Yes," said Ben. "Mr Elliott's gone away, and—"

"What?!"

"I know it sounds crazy, but it's true. You won't believe this, Boff. He's gone to stay with Mr Blake."

"What!" Boff was shocked, as predicted.

"He's going to do some building work on his house."

"So we've moved lots of Mrs Vormann's things—"

"All the valuable stuff..."

" – into Mr Elliott's house."

"What on earth for?" said Boff, mystified.

"So we can keep an eye on it, of course."

"And that's not all," said Charlotte, eyes shining, "he says we can stay in his house!"

"Charlotte asked him if we could," said Ben, grinning at her.

If Boff was excited, he didn't show it. Instead, his brain had already started searching for problems.

"I don't know that our parents'll be happy for us to be alone in Mr Elliott's house all night," he said. "If it gets burgled while we're in it, we could get hurt."

"Or tied up," said Charlotte.

"Or scared to death," said Toby.

"But they don't mind it when we stay in the Naitabal hut," Jayne protested.

"That's different," said Boff. "It's at the bottom of all the gardens—"

"Seas," corrected Toby. "You've been away from Naitabal territory for too long."

" – It's protected by the *seas* and *islands*," Boff went on, correcting his mistake, "away from human roads. So it's unlikely to be burgled. Apart from that, there's nothing in it

70

to burgle, and no one can get in because we pull the ladder up and lock it from the inside. Staying in an empty house is different. Much dodgier. Especially if people get to know it's been empty for a while."

Suddenly, everyone felt dampened by Boff's eminently practical – and horribly boring – view of the situation.

"There's five of us," said Toby. "Five of us could beat a burglar any day."

Boff turned his spectacles towards him and looked through them seriously.

"Not if there's three burglars," he said.

"Or if they've got guns or knives or something," said Charlotte, shivering.

Gloom settled over them again.

"*Unless*, of course," Boff added, beginning to sound more positive, like the Boff of old. Then he stopped.

"Yes?"

"Unless what?"

They waited patiently for the cogs of Boff's brain to turn a few more revolutions.

"Unless, of course," he went on, "we rig up some burglar-proof devices." He spoke slowly, blinking through his glasses in the bright sunshine.

"Now you're talking," said Ben. "When do we start?"

"Now, of course," said Boff. "We needn't actually tell our parents we're staying in Mr Elliott's house. We can tell them we're staying in here."

"That's deceitful," said Jayne, disgusted, but secretly hoping there was a way round it. "Naitabals never tell lies."

"Except when it's absolutely necessary," said Charlotte, reminding her of one of the best rules of Naitabal lore. "Have you forgotten your swearing-in ceremony already?"

"No, but it isn't absolutely necessary to tell a lie if we ask our parents, is it?" Jayne continued, still trying to pacify her conscience. "They might say we *can* stay in the house."

"But if you ask and they say you *can't*, it's much worse. Then you'd be going against what they said. If you don't ask, you're not being disobedient. We'll just ask if we can sleep in the Naitabal hut again. They know how safe we are in here."

Boff was still thinking.

"I know what we can do."

"What?"

"We can all stay in the Naitabal hut, at first, and have a midnight feast. Then two or three of us can go to Mr Elliott's house to keep an eye on it, and the others can stay in the hut."

"And then swap over the next night!"

"Yep!"

"I've got an even better idea," said Charlotte, grinning. "Have the midnight feast in Mr Elliott's house, then two or three stay behind, and two or three come back here to sleep."

"I like it!" said Toby.

So did the others.

"We can rig up an emergency alarm," Boff went on. "If someone breaks into the house, we just press a button, and a bell rings in here."

Boff's smile hadn't reached the outside yet, but the others felt sure that it was stirring unseen somewhere beneath the surface. He suddenly got up.

"I think we should get Mrs Vormann's book, first. My aunt was worried in case the furniture got sold."

"Did she know Mrs Vormann, then?"

"She knew her for years. They were friends when my aunt lived in our house as a girl, and they kept writing to each other when she moved away."

"Why does she want the book?"

"Mrs Vormann wrote to my aunt from hospital and told her to get it published, but not while she was alive. I don't know why. Then she died. My aunt told me to get Mr Elliott to

72

find it and post it to her when I got back home. I wrote the Naitabal letter hoping to speed things up a bit."

"What sort of book is it?" said Ben.

"It's a—" Jayne began, then stopped as she realised what she was saying. Everyone turned to look at her and she quickly turned it into a sneeze. "Itsa – tishoo!"

"It's Mrs Vormann's life story," said Boff. "It took her ten years to write."

"Wow! It must be long!" said Toby.

"Come on," said Ben. "Let's find it."

Charlotte had the privilege of turning the key in Mr Elliott's front door, and the Naitabals trooped inside. They had only been in the hall, the kitchen and the front room when they'd helped to move Mrs Vormann's furniture in. Now they discovered, after a brief safari, that the rest of Mr Elliott's house was just like his garden, his van, and his skip. The whole place, apart from the room where he slept, was stuffed with a huge variety of chattels and rubbish. Every room was crammed with old furniture, paintings, boxes, books, magazines, carpets and rugs, ornaments, jewellery, and just about everything imaginable. They were packed so full that the Naitabals could hardly open the doors, and when they did manage to open one, it was almost impossible to get inside the room to look at anything. The only way was to crawl under chairs and tables that had other things stacked ceiling-high on top of them, and negotiate the maze of legs to get to the other side.

"Should be great for a game of hide-and-seek," suggested Ben.

It was an exciting prospect, but it was something they didn't have time for yet. Boff had already started looking at walls and windows and wondering where he could fit his alarm system. The others went back down to the big front room and looked at the stack of Mrs Vormann's furniture, just as they had left it. The desk was shining as bright as ever, and the ancient typewriter sat on top, looking rather proud of itself.

They dragged Boff down, then looked inside the fourteen drawers of the desk one by one, taking it in turns. When the fourteenth (and last) drawer had been searched without any sign of Mrs Vormann's book, Boff started to look really worried.

"There weren't any other desks, were there?" he said.

"There was a small bureau," said Jayne, teasing.

"My aunt definitely said it was a big oak desk. This must be it."

They searched the drawers again. When, at last, everyone had really given up and started to look despondent (except Jayne and Charlotte), the girls nodded to each other and decided it was time to put the others out of their misery. Jayne stepped forward.

"We know where it is," she announced.

"What?"

"The book. Me and Charlotte know where the book is."

"Why on earth didn't you say so, then?"

"Because we wanted to keep it a secret until you came back," said Jayne. "It's in a secret drawer."

"What – in this desk?" said Boff, leaning on it.

"That's right." The girls grinned. "And we bet you can't find it."

"I bet we can!" Ben knelt in front of the desk, but Jayne put a restraining hand on his shoulder.

"Here's the deal. If you can find the secret drawer and get it open in five minutes, you boys stay in Mr Elliott's house tonight. If you can't, me and Charlotte have first turn."

"Deal?" said Ben, turning to the others.

Boff and Toby considered.

"Yes," said Boff at last. "But whoever stays in the house first has to get the midnight feast as well. Good news and bad news. Deal?"

It was the girls' turn to consider.

"Okay," they nodded.

Straight away, the other three unloaded all the drawers and started a detailed search of the interior of the desk. After one minute, they'd found where the secret drawer was located, after two minutes they'd found the finger hole, and after three they'd found the peg. They spent the remaining time taking it in turns to push it and pull it, and everything but twist it.

"Time's up!" shouted Charlotte. "We win!"

Then the boys stood up, intrigued and disappointed. With a curtsy, Jayne knelt in front of the desk. She smiled up at them as she pushed her right arm into the drawer hole to the right, and her left arm into the one in the middle. There was a familiar (to Jayne and Charlotte) "clonk!", then Jayne stretched a little further. Seconds later, the secret drawer came sliding out.

The boys were impressed.

"Let me have a go!"

"And me!"

Jayne pushed it back, then showed Boff, Ben, and Toby how it was done. Their curiosity was satisfied at last, and when the drawer had been removed for the fourth time, Jayne laid it on top of the desk. She took out the buff folder and handed it to Boff.

Boff opened it.

"*Spy Quest*," he read, "*by Hermine Vormann*. This must be it." A great sigh of relief went up as Boff closed the folder and tucked it under his arm. "I'll have to post it off to my aunt."

"Perhaps she was a real-life spy!" said Ben. "Let's read it before you send it," he added, making a sudden grab. "It might be exciting."

Boff swung it away, out of reach.

75

"No. I don't think we should. Mrs Vormann asked my aunt to look after it, and I don't think anyone else should touch it."

Charlotte let out a huge sigh of relief.

"Well, I'm just glad it was there," she said.

Toby looked at her, frowning.

"But Jayne said you knew about it all the time?"

"Yes, but—" Charlotte screwed up her face. "I just had a horrible feeling.... With HMS *Slugface* slithering around, putting his slimy fingers on to everything, that's all...."

"A horrible feeling of what?"

"When we saw him from the crow's nest, laughing his head off, I thought – I just thought it might be *missing*."

"Well, it isn't, silly. Anyway – why on earth would Mr Maynard want to take something like that?"

CHAPTER EIGHT

Lady in Black, Chairs in Red and Yellow

As soon as the manuscript had been rescued and Mr
Elliott's house locked again, the Naitabal domain became a
scene of intense activity.

Ben went back up to the crow's nest to keep an eye on Mrs
Vormann's house in general, and Mr Maynard in particular;
Charlotte and Jayne disappeared into Charlotte's house to
prepare for the midnight feast in Mr Elliott's house; and Boff
and Toby started a search of the Sea of Debris for things they
would need to set up an alarm system.

There was plenty of action on Pigmo Island, too. Cedric
Morgan and his sister Doris, aided by Andy and Amanda
Wilson, were all in the throes of erecting a tent, but were
being harassed from Charlotte's garden by her seven-year-
old brother. Harry had discovered his sister's bow and
arrows, and was launching them gleefully towards the
Igmopong with cries of "Fat-bang-face!" and
"Igmopongbang!" and forcing them to duck as the missiles
whizzed dangerously close to their heads. Despite dire
threats from the members of Cedric's gang, he continued to
fire at them until he had run out of arrows, and then made a
dignified but hasty retreat to the safety of his house.

After that, whenever a Naitabal passed within earshot,
Cedric announced in a loud voice, "We're sleeping out
tonight." The information floated across into the warm air
currents of the Sea of Debris, where it was completely
ignored.

"I bet *you're* not sleeping out!" he taunted, as Charlotte
and Jayne hurried by carrying handfuls of dandelions and

77

elderberries.

"I bet you're all going to sleep in boring old beds in boring old pyjamas," he jeered as Boff strode past, still clutching Mrs Vormann's precious folder under his arm.

"Yeah!" added his red-haired sister. "In your *boring* old bedrooms in your *boring* old houses!"

But Cedric's attempts at conversation met with little response, other than an occasional "Microwave your head, Cedric!" from Charlotte, or a suggestion from Jayne that they should pitch their tent in the fast lane of a motorway.

As Naitabal activity increased, however, and his own snooping grew more effective, Cedric worked out what they were up to.

"I bet you're sleeping in Mr Elliott's house!" he shouted. This goaded them into responding, and he knew then that he had hit the bull's-eye.

"No, we're not!" came the slightly defensive reply. "We're sleeping in the Naitabal hut."

"I bet you're not! I bet – !"

At that point a well-aimed water-bomb sailed over the fence, struck Cedric neatly in the face, and flopped down, soaking his shirt. The Naitabals didn't hear much from the Igmopong after that. Before long they seemed to disappear altogether.

"They usually fight back," murmured Toby. "They must be planning something stupid instead."

He and Boff were looking for wire by this time, and found some with an ancient coating of heavy, metallic lead.

"Don't touch it," said Boff. "It's poisonous. It ought to be thrown away."

"It has been thrown away," Toby reminded him, logically. "It's in with Mr Elliott's junk."

All the plastic-coated wire they could find was in short lengths, none of them much longer than a few metres.

"It has to be weatherproof," said Boff. "We'll need special

78

joiners and insulating tape."

They found some ancient bell pushes but no electric bells, so Toby cycled to the local shops before they closed and bought two buzzers and a roll of tape. By the time he got back, Boff had had some luck. He had discovered a whole reel of household cable with four different coloured wires inside.

"Just what we need," said Boff. "Four wires."

They collected some tools, and while Toby screwed a bell-push and a buzzer inside the Naitabal hut beneath the north window, Boff drew a diagram. It looked something like this:

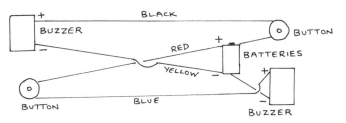

They poked the end of the cable in through a small knot hole and connected the four coloured wires the way Boff had drawn them. They wound the cable along one rope of the three-rope bridge until they reached Boff Island, then trailed it along the fence on Boff's side, tacking it in place with staples. They led the wire up the lilac tree and on to a branch that pointed towards Mr Elliott's house. Toby fetched a ladder and pushed the rest of the cable into the top of the bathroom window.

They installed the second bell-push and buzzer in Mr Elliott's house, on a wooden block that could be moved from room to room. Toby went off to fit a set of rechargeable batteries in the Naitabal hut, and he and Boff made final connections at each end.

Toby pressed the button in the Naitabal hut. Inside Mr

Elliott's house, there was a satisfying buzz from the wooden block. Boff pressed the button at his end, and Toby gave him a thumbs-up sign through the tree-house window.

"One buzz for help, two buzzes for emergency help, and three buzzes for call the police," said Boff, when Toby returned.

Most of the other preparations were done, and the Naitabals, all except Ben, separated to their homes to have their evening meals.

Ben had decided to get something else ready that they would need the following day. First, he fetched the wooden kitchen chair they had used to hoist up the tree for their abortive attempt at a crow's nest. After that, he delved under the tarpaulin again, pulled out another chair from the set, took them both up to Mr Elliott's house, and stood them on the patch of long grass by the back door. A separate search produced two rusty tins of paint, one bright red, and one bright yellow. Finally, armed with an old screwdriver and a brush whose bristles were as stiff as the handle, he settled down to make his preparations.

He opened the tin of bright red paint with the screwdriver, dipped in the brush, and started daubing the first chair with it. Gradually the bristles began to soften. When the chair was garish red all over, he opened the pot of bright yellow paint and started applying it to the other chair. About half way through, Cedric Morgan's head appeared over the next door fence.

"Oo-er, what horrible colours!" he said sarcastically. "I suppose you're going to put them in your tree-house, are you?"

Ben recognised the oily voice and didn't bother to look up.

"They're for the Challenge," he said, and carried on painting.

"Oh – you've thought of something, have you? It's taken you long enough. I thought we'd probably be grown up by

80

the time you thought of anything."

"Well, you couldn't think of anything."

"What's it going to be? See who can paint a chair the fastest? It's a bit mean you practising, and not giving us a chance."

"Which colour do you prefer?" said Ben, ignoring Cedric's sarcastic whine. "Yellow or red? Yellow suits your character better, of course."

Cedric wasted a belligerent stare on Ben's back.

"No, it doesn't," he said. "We'll have red – for danger."

"Suit yourself."

"When do we get a chance to practise?"

"Practise what?"

"Whatever it is?"

"You won't need any practice. Just a red chair. You hide the red chair and we hide the yellow chair. We have to find yours, and you have to find ours. Whoever finds the others' chair first, wins."

"Poo! Is that all? Not much of a challenge. We could just bury ours, and you'd *never* find it."

Ben condescended to look across to the fence for the first time, and saw Cedric's chubby face perched on the top with a set of fingers holding on each side.

"There'll be rules," he said shortly. "We'll meet before the challenge in the morning, and I'll tell everyone what they can do and what they can't do. Then we'll have your boat for a week."

"Huh! We'll have your tree-house for a week, you mean!"

With these final formalities ended, Cedric disappeared, and Ben finished off the yellow chair.

As he was wiping the brush on the grass, he heard a woman's voice.

"Excuse me, is this Mr Elliott's house?"

Ben stopped. The voice came round the corner from near the skip, and he stretched his neck and saw her. She had black hair and she was wearing a very smart black skirt and jacket, which stood out starkly against the yellow of the skip. She looked about thirty, and she was smiling at him with a warm smile and bright, humorous eyes. He liked her straight away.

"Yes," he said. "This is Mr Elliott's house."

"I couldn't get an answer. Is he your father?"

Ben flushed.

"No. He hasn't got any children. He's not married."

"Oh, sorry. Do you know if he's in?"

"No, he's not."

"Do you know when he might be back?"

In spite of the sunny smile and the friendly eyes, Ben didn't want to say too much. He knew it was foolish to tell strangers if a house was empty for long – or anyone, for that matter. They might be burglars, or if they weren't they might mention it to someone else, and *they* might be burglars.

Ben hadn't answered, and the lady in black smiled even more.

"Not saying in case I'm a burglar?" she said, and Ben felt shocked at having his thoughts read. "Very sensible, and I don't blame you a bit. Perhaps I'd better explain who I am." She delved into a pocket and produced a little card.

Ben took it and read:

JULIE GOULD
SOLICITOR

The words were printed in gold on a black background.

"As you can see," she explained, "I'm a solicitor."

"Oh."

"I'm acting in connection with someone called Mrs Vormann, who died recently – have you heard of her?"

"Yes," said Ben.

82

"I understand that Mr Elliott is one of her – er—"

"Executors," said Ben.

"Oh!" Another smile, this time of surprise. "You are well informed. Yes – looking after her estate. That's why I need to talk to him. Can you help?"

Ben didn't think it would matter, saying anything. After all, she was a solicitor, and her smile was particularly nice.

"He's gone away," he said.

"How long for?"

"Two or three weeks."

"Oh. Oh dear. Do you know where he's gone?"

"No," said Ben. He knew, of course, that he'd gone to stay with Mr Blake, but he hadn't the faintest idea where Mr Blake lived, and had no inclination to find out.

"No," he said again.

"Is there someone who does know where he's gone?"

"No. He's not friendly with anyone, much."

The sweet smile grew wide again, and the bright eyes sparkled.

"I called at Mrs Vormann's house earlier. The man next door told me some of her furniture had been moved into Mr Elliott's house. Is that right?"

"Yes," said Ben. "We helped."

"That was nice of you. Did you move much?"

Despite the nice smiles, Ben started to feel uncomfortable again about the detailed questions, and retracted into silence.

"You're quite right," said the lady in black. "I'm being far too nosy. I'll just have to wait until Mr Elliott gets back, that's all. Two to three weeks, you said?"

"Yes."

"I don't suppose you know who's looking after the house in the meantime?"

Ben hesitated again, feeling that he had already said far too much.

"No," he said, at last.

83

The lady thanked him with a last flashing smile, then walked across the road to a brand new black sports coupé. The engine roared into life, and she was gone. Ben watched the car until it rounded the curve, then walked home, deep in thought.

CHAPTER NINE

In the Dark, Dark House

There was no moon, and the sky's dark complexion was freckled with stars. Shadows of sleeping-bags were huddled at tree-house windows steamed with the breath of five warm Naitabals. They were all excited and ready for their midnight feast, watching and waiting for the moment when it would be safe for Jayne and Charlotte to make their way to Mr Elliott's house and set it up. When it was set up – and only then – they would use the buzzer to call the boys to go across and join them.

Ben had reported the visit of the lady in black. No one had any ideas about what she might have wanted, but they all agreed that Ben had done the right thing by not telling her too much.

"What time is it?"

"Eleven thirty."

"Is HMS *Slugface still* there?"

"Still there," whispered Toby, who was manning the telescope. "I don't trust him."

"What's he doing?"

"Shuffling his heap of papers."

"What about the Pigmo Lightship?" asked Jayne.

Boff looked at the ghostly hump of tent that was visible on Pigmo Island.

"Just a faint glow," he said. "But nothing moving. We'd better go really quietly if we don't want them to wake up and start shouting and telling the whole world that we're going to Mr Elliott's house."

It was just the Naitabals' luck that Cedric Morgan and his

gang should decide to spend the night in their tent. (Their tree-house was no fit place for spending a night.) Ever since the Naitabals had watched them crawl under the canvas at dusk, the Igmopong had been unusually quiet. Only the light from a single torch and static, unrecognisable shadows gave any clue to their presence at all.

"I wonder if they're up to something?" said Toby.

"They're probably all asleep," said Charlotte. "They'd never switch off their torch, whatever happened."

"Why?"

"Because they'd be afraid to wake up in the dark, of course."

All around, one by one, lights were going out, but not Mr Maynard's. There was an upstairs light on in Cedric Morgan's house, and a downstairs one in Charlotte's. At one of Boff's windows they could see the luminous flashings of a television screen, and next to it Mr Elliott's rooftop hugged the edge of the woods that lay beyond in a black and ominous silence.

"He's turned his light out!" said Toby suddenly.

The others turned to look. Where there had been a small yellow glow on Slug Island, there was now only darkness.

"Good. That's him out of the way," said Charlotte. "We can go soon."

"That's funny," whispered Toby. He had abandoned the telescope, and was looking directly out of the south window.

"What's funny?"

"Mr Maynard's upstairs light hasn't come on. No bathroom light, nothing."

"What's so funny about that?" said Ben.

"Well, if he's gone to bed, he should be turning upstairs lights on, shouldn't he? That's what he usually does. You see the downstairs lights go off and the upstairs ones come on."

"He's probably saving electricity. Sitting at his desk,

86

staring into nothingness."

"There's something weird about that man," Jayne commented.

"I still think one of us should go with the girls," said Boff to the others.

Charlotte's and Jayne's eyes flashed in the shadows.

"Why?" they hissed. "Because you think you're better than us? Or stronger? Or can't be frightened?"

Boff seemed taken aback, and answered weakly, "Just strength in numbers, that's all."

"We're only going to set out the feast and then call you on the buzzer," said Jayne. "If anything's wrong, we just use the alarm anyway. What could be easier?"

Charlotte looked at her watch again.

"Anyway,"she said, "it's twenty-five to twelve. We can go now."

Mr Maynard sat in his chair in the yellow glow of the desk lamp, gazing at the blackness outside that pressed against his study window. Though his eyes stared into darkness, there was a satisfied glow in whatever it was that passed for his heart. He had tried very hard to buy the desk from Mr Elliott, but in the end it hadn't been necessary. He had helped them to move the rest of the furniture, and then he had helped himself to the spare key to Mr Elliott's house. It had been stupidly left under a flowerpot outside the back door. People would never learn, he thought. They only got what they deserved.

He glanced at the travelling clock on his desk. Eleven thirty. Time. With a look of grim determination, he leaned forward and pressed the button on his desk lamp. The black shadows that had been lurking threateningly outside crowded in and filled the study. Slowly, as his eyes adjusted to the darkness, he could see the silhouettes of the few trees that lined the side of his garden, and of the huge oak that stood a few gardens away.

Ten minutes later, he stood up. Fondling the key in his pocket, he allowed himself a brief smile, then made his way quietly through the dark house.

Cedric Morgan checked the luminous hands of his watch and silently signalled to the others that it was time to go. Leaving the single torch glowing inside the tent, they opened the flaps that faced away from the Naitabal hut and crept up the garden on their bellies. They kept as near to the fence as they could get without actually going through the flowerbed. When they drew level with Mr Elliott's house, Cedric felt for the three loose fencing panels, then swung them out of the way so that they could all squeeze through.

At the side of Mr Elliott's house was a small window with iron bars across. It was just below ground level, and it was set into a niche in the path. Cedric knew it led into Mr Elliott's cellar. He'd made sure it was unlocked earlier in the day when he had wandered around the house unseen during the furniture removals. He pulled at the frame, and the window swung outwards. They went in backwards, feeling the way with their feet.

When they were all inside, Cedric switched on his torch. The floor of the cellar was brick-lined and damp, and the walls were stained and crumbly-white. Over their heads they could see the floorboards of the room above.

"*Roolf*!" he said, trying to impress the others with his new backwards language.

"Do you mean 'roof'?" said Doris in a belligerent whisper.

Cedric ignored her and waved the torch at the wooden steps.

"*Spets*!" he said.

"It's no good talking your wonderful Cedric Language if no one else understands it!" hissed Doris. "Talk English!"

"There are the steps!" he whispered.

"You don't say!" muttered Doris.

His motley band were eager for adventure and, despite Doris's complaints, quite impressed so far. They scampered after him, weaving from side to side like dolphins following a boat.

Cedric climbed up the little wooden flight, folding himself double near the top, then shone his beam upwards. He pushed on the little wooden trap-door and let out a quiet sigh of relief as it yielded. He then pushed it up on its hinges until it rested against the wall above.

Now he was inside the cupboard in Mr Elliott's front room. He hoped that no one had locked it since his previous visit. They hadn't. He switched off his torch, then pushed at the door, which swung open without a squeak. He stood up and stepped into the room. There was hardly any light coming through the windows, but his eyes quickly grew accustomed to the dark outlines of Mrs Vormann's furniture. Doris emerged behind him, followed by Andy and Amanda.

"This is a real adventure, isn't it?" Cedric breathed, pleased with his own cleverness.

The others agreed that it was.

"Upstairs, first," he whispered.

Carefully, they felt their way past the obstacles and crossed the room to the hall. Then up the stairs. Cedric signalled to Andy and Amanda to close the front bedroom curtains, then switched on his torch again. Its beam fell on the white cable that came in through the bathroom window, through the bathroom, across the landing, and into Mr Elliott's room, where they stood. He shone the torch on the wooden block where it ended, with Boff and Toby's contraptions screwed to it.

"What's it for?" said Andy. He reached out to press the button, but Cedric's hand shot out like a frog's tongue and stopped him just in time.

"Don't touch the button, idiot! It'll ring the bell in Ben

Tuffin's tree-house! They'll all come swarming over like wasps!"

"That's what it's *for*, stupid!" spat Doris. She was secretly relieved that Andy had got the telling off, because she'd been just about to press it herself.

Cedric smirked cunningly in the glow of the torch.

"If we disconnect the wires, it won't work," he said, pulling a small screwdriver from his pocket. "I brought this so we could do it. They won't be able to signal for help."

"That's right," said Doris. "But if you disconnect the wires, they'll *see* that the wires are disconnected, and they'll join 'em up again."

"Yeah," said Andy.

"And then they *will* be able to signal for help," put in Amanda.

"Well, I'll swap some wires over, then," Cedric conceded.

In the faint yellow torchlight, Doris looked alarmed.

"Well, don't touch those two together," she said. She stubbed a blunt finger at the red and blue wires that were connected to the push button. "'Cos that's what happens when you press the button."

"I know that!" said Cedric, lying. He didn't know the first thing about electricity, and he was secretly pleased that she'd told him. "I'll just swap the black and blue ones." Then, doubtfully, "Will I get a shock?"

"They're only connected to little torch batteries, stupid," said Doris. She wasn't actually a hundred per cent certain herself. She watched, fascinated, half expecting her brother to light up and burst into flames.

Three minutes later, however, the job was safely done.

"Now they'll *never* get help," said Cedric, satisfied with his own cunning. He slipped the screwdriver back into his pocket. "Even if they press it till their fingers fall off."

"What do we do next?" said Doris.

"Hide, of course," said Cedric. "If they're supposed to be

having a midnight feast, they'll be here any minute." He threw open – or rather, tried to throw open – one of the upstairs bedroom doors, but found that its movement was impeded by a mass of furniture on the other side. He tried another room and met with much the same result.

"You'll have to hide in there!" he said, pointing through the gap and under the furniture.

"How am I supposed to do that?" complained Doris, shining her torch into the jungle of wooden legs. "It's like one of them mangrove swamp places."

"Just crawl in, and shut up complaining," said Cedric, still feeling strongly in command.

Doris crawled in, and Cedric closed the door. He ordered Amanda to crawl into the first room they had looked at, and closed that door, too.

"And what do we do next?" demanded Doris's disembodied voice in an aggressive whisper. Her question was further muffled by a mattress, a settee, and several occasional chairs.

"Wait for my command," Cedric hissed airily, but without the slightest idea of what his command might be, or what she was supposed to do when she heard it. Luckily, all three of them had been so impressed with his route into Mr Elliott's house, that his standing as leader was still high enough for them not to argue further.

He stationed Andy in the cupboard under the stairs, and only then did he start to admit to himself that he had formed no definite plan of action. Other than hoping to spoil whatever the Naitabals were up to, he hadn't the first idea how to achieve it.

He had thought of haunting them, but he couldn't work out how to do it convincingly. It was all very well to rattle chains (even if he had any), or creak doors, or make ghostly groans and footsteps, but it only needed the flash of a Naitabal torch for his game to be discovered. As most of the rooms were stacked to the ceiling with furniture, it would also be impossible to move around much, or hide in a hurry.

Hoping that some opportunity would present itself, Cedric hid himself downstairs, in the front room cupboard that led back down to the cellar. He waited, trying to nudge his brain into gear.

It seemed that he waited for years. But only ten minutes passed before he heard the sound of a key – several keys, in fact – being tried one after another in the front door. After that, he heard the door open and close, and the lightest trace of footsteps in the hall, coming into the front room. He started to tremble as he saw stray torchlight illuminating his own trainers under the cupboard door. Then he heard the sound of desk drawers being opened, searched, closed. He tried to stoop down quietly and apply his eye to the keyhole, but he couldn't see anything other than vague shadows in the dim beam of the torch.

Almost immediately, there was the sound of a key in the front door again. But the snooper's torch was extinguished, and he heard footfalls near the desk, followed by a faint rustle of clothing. Now there were footsteps in the hall, whispered voices, and feet ascending the stairs.

Jayne and Charlotte stepped out of their warm sleeping-bags and rolled them up ready for the short journey across the Sea of Debris. Next, they opened the trap-door and lowered the mysterious boxes that contained the midnight feast. With a speed honed by many practice runs, they silently lowered the rope ladder, then escaped to the ground. There was no sound or movement from the Igmopong Lightship as they crept towards Mr Elliott's house.

They reached his front door without incident, and Charlotte quietly inserted the Yale key and turned it. The door opened and they slipped inside. They carried the boxes and sleeping-bags to Mr Elliott's room. They had decided to sleep there as it was the only place free from stacks of furniture. The curtains were already closed, and they went to a window each and carefully peeped through the gaps in the thick velvet.

"Boff and Toby must have closed the curtains," Charlotte whispered, then thought nothing more of it.

After a glance in both directions along the dark road outside, she and Jayne closed the chinks again, and only then dared to turn on their torches.

"Here's the emergency buzzer," said Charlotte, pointing down to where it lay. Secretly, she felt relieved that the others were only the push of a button away.

"One buzz to come over, two buzzes for emergency help, and three to call the police," chanted Jayne. "Not that I think we'll need it," she added bravely. "Apart from the one buzz to call them when the midnight feast is ready."

They were just about to start unloading the boxes, when Charlotte noticed something lying on Mr Elliott's big bed.

"Oh, Boff!" she moaned.

Jayne followed the line of Charlotte's torch and saw what she had seen. The folder from the secret drawer of Mrs Vormann's desk was lying near the pillow. Charlotte reached out and pulled it towards them.

"Look! It's Mrs Vormann's book! Boff forgot to take it home and post it!"

"He was carrying it around all afternoon. He must have left it here when they were fixing the buzzers."

Suddenly, a vehicle hurtled by on the road outside, making them both jump. Its lights flew across the ceiling from one side of the room to the other, then it was gone. It hadn't stopped, but it had the effect of unsettling them. There seemed to be an eerie silence, then, that hadn't been there before. They whispered very quietly, but even their own whispers seemed ghostly and unreal. They made another attempt to unpack the midnight feast.

Jayne lifted out an oblong raspberry jelly, quivering on a dish.

"We'll cut that into slices and make jelly sandwiches," she said.

But it was the only thing that ever got lifted out. Moments later, they both heard another sound – a sound that turned the blood in their veins to something cold and solid, like the raspberry jelly.

It came from downstairs, and it was the sound of a key being turned in the back door.

CHAPTER TEN

Things That Go Tap in the Night

The girls snapped off their torches and held their heads close together in the darkness, listening. Already their hearts had started racing. The sound of the key turning in the lock was followed by the tiny squeak of a door opening, and a muffled click as it was gently closed again.

"It can't be the others," said Jayne in a voice so hushed that Charlotte, right next to her, could hardly hear it. "Our key's for the front door."

Charlotte made her own voice as small as she could.

"We haven't signalled that we're ready yet, either." Then she added, "Perhaps it's Mr Elliott back," but she didn't really think for a second that it was.

They could both feel their own hearts thumping in their ears, making it difficult to listen. Not daring to move, they strained for more sounds from downstairs. Now there was a faint footfall in the hallway, a slight knock – was it a shoe against a piece of furniture?

Carefully, Charlotte slid away from Jayne. Her fingers reached out in the blackness towards the floor, trying to find the buzzer board. She found the cable. Gingerly, her fingers traced it along. There was another noise from downstairs, another door creaking open – the front room directly beneath them. Charlotte's finger closed on the piece of wood and groped for the button. Then, holding her breath, she tried to calm the racing throb of the heartbeat in her ears. She pressed the button once – good and long – twice – another good long push. The boys wouldn't be asleep, of course. They were ready for the midnight feast. They'd come straight away.

She eased herself back towards Jayne.

"Done it," she whispered. "Two pushes."

Jayne felt relieved.

"They'll be here in no time. What shall we do?"

"Stay here. Let the others catch them red-handed. We'll go down when we hear them coming in."

Seconds of silence passed, followed by a few strange clicks, and a few more muffled bumps. Then they heard the last thing they ever expected to hear. It started slowly, and gradually increased in speed. It was the ghostly sound of the tapping of a typewriter, hanging in the dark air, haunting them. They heard the slapping of its metal on to paper, the little "ting" of its bell, and the whirring thump as its carriage scuttled back to begin another line.

"It's Mrs Vormann's typewriter!" whispered Charlotte. "Someone's using it!"

There was no mistaking the rhythm of the sounds. "Tap, tap, tap-tap-tap, tap, tap, tap-tap, tap-tap, tap-tap-tap, tap-tap, tap-tap-tap, ting!" over and over again.

"Let's go and look!" said Jayne.

For once, Charlotte wasn't sure of herself.

"Who can be typing at this time of night?"

"How should I know?"

"And why come into Mr Elliott's house to do it?"

"Perhaps they haven't got one of their own."

"How did they know Mrs Vormann's typewriter was here, then?"

"I don't know! I'm Jayne Croft, not Claire Voyant!"

Charlotte smiled a grim, humourless smile, and then made up her mind.

"Come on, then."

Carefully, they eased themselves into an upright position, hoping the floorboards wouldn't squeak.

"Tap-tap, tap-tap, tap-tap-tap-tap-tap, tap, tap, tap-tap, tap-

tap, tap-tap-tap, tap, ting!"

They both felt the cold fingers of night around them, groping next to their skin, making them shiver. Their eyes had grown accustomed to the dark again, and Charlotte leaned down to where the end of the white cable lay. She found the push button, and pressed it twice more, hard.

"For luck!" she whispered. Then she straightened up again, and added, "Can you remember if any of the floorboards creaked?"

"Don't know. Don't think so."

"Tap-tap, tap-tap, tap-tap-tap-tap-tap, tap, tap, tap-tap, tap-tap, tap-tap-tap, tap, ting!"

"We'll have to take a chance."

Slowly, carefully, every muscle tense with the strain, they eased their way across the floor.

"Tap-tap, tap-tap, tap-tap-tap-tap-tap, tap, tap, tap-tap, tap-tap, tap-tap-tap, tap, ting!"

Charlotte was in front, and pulled the door gently towards them. It didn't make the slightest sound as it opened, but the tapping downstairs suddenly stopped. The girls froze in their tracks. Now there was the sound of paper being wound off the carriage. Then hurried footsteps through the room below, and along to the kitchen. They saw – only for a moment – the flash of a torch and a dark moving shadow. They still dared not move. The kitchen door squeaked open, closed again, a key turned in the lock.

"Quick! See if we can see who it is! You go to the front!" Charlotte yapped the commands, in much less of a whisper now that the mysterious intruder had gone, and hurried in the darkness to the back bedroom. But she had forgotten the furniture. It was stacked high to the doorway, and there was no way she could get to the window to look out of it in less than a few minutes. She turned and followed Jayne to the front of the house instead.

Now they were both at the big curtained windows of Mr

Elliott's room, drawing back the heavy velvet and peering out into the dark street below. The same shadowy figure emerged from the front of the house. It turned and sailed northwards along the Straits of Brunswick and submerged into the shadows like an enemy U-boat.

"Where are the others?" screamed Charlotte, suddenly furious. "Fat lot of use having an alarm system if they don't even bother to answer it!"

"They'll never catch him now!" said Jayne.

"Come on! Let's find out what's going on!"

The torches were brought back into use, and within seconds the girls were hurrying down the stairs. Jayne shone her beam on the old typewriter that stood darkly on the desk, just as they had last seen it. Who had typed on it? What had they typed? But it just sat there, dumb and unhelpful, sharing its secret with no one.

Charlotte was at the front door, and Jayne hurried to catch up, following her out into the night. They clambered over the rubbish, round the skip, and down the obstacle-strewn path. There was still no sign of Ben, Boff or Toby, no torches coming up the path to meet them, no hushed "Hi!"s in the darkness. Above them, in the Naitabal hut, a weak, yellow light was glowing.

Charlotte, still furious, picked up a handful of gravel and flung it up towards the Naitabal bell. It rattled on the under-side of the floor. The bell sang with a bright, clear voice in the still night air. Three Naitabal silhouettes rose up at the windows like zombies and stared into the darkness. The yellow light went out, and the north window inched open.

"Who's there?" Ben's voice, hushed.

"It's us, you loonies!" Charlotte's hissing reply, mouse quiet, but snake angry. "Let us in!"

The window closed, the trap-door opened, and the rope ladder came looping down. The girls climbed up.

"What about the feast?" complained Toby as soon as their

heads appeared at the trap-door. "We're starving."

Inside, Charlotte and Jayne gave rein to their feelings.

"Feast! Never mind the midnight feast!"

"We had an intruder..."

"We pressed the button – twice – and where were you lot?"

"We were in deadly danger, and all you did was—"

Boff was holding up a hand.

"Hold on, hold on, hold on," he said three times, getting through with the third one. "We were listening for you all the time. Did you say you pressed the button?"

"Yes!"

"Nothing happened here," put in Ben.

"And all this time we're starving," repeated Toby.

"We did press it – twice—"

"And you had an *intruder*?"

"Yes! He came in the back door, did some typing, and went away again..."

"Did some *what*?"

"Typing. There was me and Jayne, all alone in Mr Elliott's room with this *maniac* in the house downstairs, pressing the buzzer for all we were worth, and thinking 'Oh, great, the other three'll be racing to our rescue any second now,' and all the time you're just sitting in here dreaming the night away!"

"Calm down, for goodness sake," said Boff, calm himself. "It's obvious what's happened."

"What?"

"Well – the buzzer didn't work."

"Oh, brilliant! I thought you were going to explain why someone would go into Mr Elliott's house just to do a bit of typing! There was me and Jayne being *murdered*, and all you can say is that the life-saving buzzer, the brilliant device that would make it safe to stay in Mr Elliott's house, that you spent *hours* putting together, and *ages* so-called testing, didn't work!"

After this satisfying outburst, Charlotte calmed down a little more. Between them, she and Jayne related the story of what had happened, and the others asked questions until they could visualise the whole scene as if they had been there themselves.

"And you did something else wrong, as well," added Jayne accusingly.

"What?"

"You left Mrs Vormann's manuscript behind!"

"*Oh, iddle-feng!*" said Boff, and clapped a hand to his glasses. "I forgot!"

"Can't we go to Mr Elliott's house and have the feast now?" pleaded Toby. "The insides of my stomach are beginning to stick together."

"It's my own fault," Boff went on. "I meant to take it home, but I kept putting it down where I was working, and I clean forgot about it."

"That's all very well," Toby persisted, "*but shall we eat?*"

This time his suggestion was greeted with general agreement, and they prepared to start their journey up to the house. Four of them went down the ladder, leaving Boff to lock up and go out through the roof as usual. As the four made their way stealthily through the Sea of Debris, there was a small commotion coming from the Pigmo Lightship. Until that moment, it had been deathly quiet all evening. Now there were sounds of whisperings and sniggerings and gigglings. Torch beams played erratically across the canvas on the inside.

The Naitabals ignored it all and walked on.

But inside Mr Elliott's house, their midnight feast had disappeared, and Mrs Vormann's folder had gone, too.

CHAPTER ELEVEN

Ight-ning

Cedric began to wish he had hidden in the bedroom above so that he could hear what the voices were saying. Thinking that all the intruders had gone upstairs, he carefully eased open the cupboard door and crept out in the darkness. He had just reached the back of the wall-high stack of furniture that the Naitabals had helped to bring in, when there was yet another unexpected sound. This time it was a key in the back door.

The murmured voices and creaking floorboards in the room above stopped immediately. It was then that Cedric knew that the latest caller was not another Naitabal. He ducked down behind the bulky desk and waited, trying to hold his breath. When he did breathe, it was too noisy. He opened his mouth wide and could taste the dust as he took big, quiet gasps.

The back door clicked shut, and through the knee-hole of the desk he saw the shapes of torchlight dancing in the doorway and a pair of dark trousers and big black shoes. For a moment he nearly cried out in panic as the little beam flashed across his knees, but it only lasted a split second as the figure approached the desk.

Then came the unexpected sound of a piece of paper being wound into a typewriter. Then the tap-tap of its keys and the "ting" of its little bell as it reached the end of each line. Cedric stayed motionless, hardly daring to breathe at all, and wishing he could see the face of the person, but realising it was impossible without being seen himself.

After an age, the typing stopped, and he heard a faintly

whispered "That's it!" The paper was wound out, and the dancing beam of light retreated once more to the doorway. Footsteps sounded in the hall and through the kitchen. The back door opened and closed, and the key turned in the lock.

Instantly, there were voices in the room upstairs again. Urgent voices and running feet. Then a pause, more voices. He recognised them. Charlotte and Jayne. Their feet running down the stairs again, out through the front door, and the front door closing. Silence.

Slowly, Cedric got up from his crouched position, felt his way under the desk to the doorway and shouted up the stairs as he started to climb them.

"Now!"

He switched on his torch and watched as Doris emerged, crumpled and dust-ridden, crawling on her front from one of the back bedrooms.

"What do you mean, 'Now!'?" she said, sounding fed up. "It's a bit late, ain't it? They've all gone!"

But Cedric had reached the front bedroom, and his torch was already shining on the boxes that contained the Naitabals' midnight feast.

He spoke in a self-confident voice, as if he had planned the whole thing from beginning to end: "Oh, yes, they've gone, all right. But their midnight feast hasn't." Then he added in a smarmy voice, "Yet!"

"They've left a folder as well," said Amanda. "Shall we take it?"

"Show me," commanded Cedric.

Amanda handed him the buff folder, and Cedric flipped it open to see what was inside. He pulled the first sheet out and looked at it.

"*Spy Quest*, by Hermine Vormann," he read. "It's something they brought from her house."

"Let's take it," said Andy.

"No-o," said Cedric. "It's Mrs Vormann's. We'd better

102

not touch anything of Mrs Vormann's. It's only Naitabal things we want."

He handed the folder back to Amanda, and she tossed it on to Mr Elliott's bed.

"Put that jelly back in the box," ordered Cedric, "and let's get out of here."

"They were goin' to slice it up and put it in sandwiches," said Amanda. "I heard 'em."

"That's what we'll do, then."

They clambered down the stairs with the boxes, and made their way round the furniture in the front room to reach the cupboard.

But none of them saw the tall human shadow that lurked in the corner behind the door.

Five Naitabals stood in a line in Mr Elliott's bedroom, and five torches illuminated the floor space where the boxes full of midnight feast ought to have been. In a daze, Charlotte flashed her light around the room as if the midnight feast might have moved itself, or as if Mrs Vormann's folder might have jumped off the bed without assistance, and into a corner, just for fun. But her beam fell only on Mr Elliott's furniture, Mr Elliott's empty bed, and Mr Elliott's empty floor.

"Someone tell me we've fallen asleep, and this is just a dream," moaned Jayne.

"You haven't fallen asleep," Ben confirmed. "And it isn't a dream. It's a nightmare."

"There's only one explanation for everything," said Boff.

"What?"

"The Igmopong, of course," put in Ben, before Boff could say it.

"That's why they've been so quiet for so long," said Toby. "We should have learnt by now."

"They weren't in their tent at all," said Ben. "They were in

103

here, waiting for the girls."

"Didn't you realise it was them?" said Toby, turning to Jayne and Charlotte.

"You'd never have thought it was them," said Jayne, with spirit. "It was so ghostly. And anyway, we saw a shadowy figure sailing along the Straits. That wasn't an Igmopong."

"Unless they were piggy-backed and wearing a long coat, or something," said Ben. "That could look good in the dark."

"It must have been them," Boff repeated. "No one else would have taken the food. And they've taken Mrs Vormann's manuscript."

"But how could they have got in?" said Ben.

"They must have had a back door key," said Charlotte. "We heard it."

"I bet Cedric found a spare one when we were moving the furniture in. He was hanging around a lot."

"Crafty devil!" said Jayne.

"Didn't you hear them enjoying themselves when we came up through the Sea of Debris?" said Boff.

"Let's go and get it back," said Toby. His eye sockets were thrown into deep shadow in the pale torchlight, and made him look like Frankenstein's monster seeking revenge. "Let's go and pull their tent down before they've eaten everything."

"Yes, let's," Jayne encouraged him. "It's all they deserve. They can sleep out in the cold."

"They've probably finished the food by now," said Ben. "But we could still pull their tent down."

He and Toby started for the door, and the girls turned to follow them as well. Boff didn't move. The others sensed his opposition even before they heard the sharp "No!" behind them. It was said in such a commanding voice that they all stopped dead. They turned. The reflection of their torches shone on Boff's glasses, masking his eyes and making him look almost sinister in the half-darkness.

"Why not?" said Toby. "It's all they deserve."

"Because we can't, that's why not."

"Yes, we can. It's easy. We just pull out the pegs and it falls down."

"It's not as simple as that." Boff was deadly serious – much more than any of them could remember seeing him before. "If we go anywhere near their tent at half past midnight, they'll squeal like the Pigmos they are, and shout and scream and yell, and all our parents will hear it. They'll guess what's going on, and the next thing you know we'll be banned from sleeping in the tree-house. They'll say 'See – we trusted you. But all you did was mess around in the Morgans' garden half the night. You pulled down their tent and woke up half the neighbourhood.'"

The others stood frozen like shop dummies, staring at Boff. Slowly, they began to calm down as one by one they realised that he was probably right.

"And Cedric Morgan *knows* we can't touch him tonight, as well," Boff went on. "He's cunning like that. Seems to know what he can get away with, and what he can't."

"Or he's just lucky," said Toby.

"We must be able to do *something*," said Jayne, her impatience rising again. "We can't just let them get clean away with it."

"And what about Mrs Vormann's book?" said Charlotte. "We'll have to get that back."

"Yes," said Boff. "That's important."

"How about a surprise attack in the morning?" suggested Ben.

"They'll have eaten the food by then," said Jayne.

"Well, at least we could get the book."

"Not if he's hidden it. Even Cedric wouldn't be so stupid as to take it into the tent with him."

Boff heaved a deep sigh, not satisfied.

105

"You're right, Charlotte," he said. "I'll have to get the book. My aunt trusted me to get it, and I did get it – once – and it's my fault we've lost it."

"What are you going to do?"

"Well, first, I don't think any of us should sleep here tonight. Sorry, but it's too dangerous with the alarm not working. The Igmopong must have cut the wires."

"Why do they always have to interfere?" Charlotte complained viciously. "Why can't they do their own things instead of just spoiling everyone else's?"

"Because they're too stupid to think of anything of their own," said Ben.

Before long, they all felt tiredness weighing down on them. Ben yawned first, setting Jayne off, then Charlotte, then Toby. A yawning contest followed. Boff was still thinking about Mrs Vormann's book, and pushed past them to start making his way downstairs. The others followed, waiting in the hall while he bolted the back door from the inside.

"At least that'll stop the Igmopong getting in tomorrow night," he said.

They locked the front door, and a dispirited procession started to make its way through the Sea of Debris. Jayne and Charlotte were carrying their sleeping-bags, feeling robbed of their night as pioneers looking after the house and Mrs Vormann's furniture.

They reached a point opposite the Igmopong Lightship, and Boff gestured for everyone to keep quiet while he approached it. The tent was still glowing with the light of dim torches, and it was still emitting low murmurs, the sounds of eating, and occasional bouts of helpless sniggering.

"Cedric!" Boff's voice hung in the cold night air. Immediately afterwards there was silence from the tent. No answer.

"Cedric! Are you awake?"

There were sounds of shuffling, a hissed instruction from Doris. Then Cedric's voice emerged, defiant.

"If you come anywhere near us, we'll scream the garden down," he said.

"I don't see how you can scream a garden down," said Boff calmly. "Scream a house down, perhaps, but it's a bit difficult with a garden."

"Well, we'll scream, anyway, and my parents'll come, and you'll all get told off."

"That's all right, Cedric. We know you've got our food. You tricked us fair and square. It was a really clever trick, doing the typewriter like that. Had us fooled."

Ben and Toby turned in the darkness behind him, pretending to throw up.

"Did you *really* think it was clever?" said Cedric the Gullible, sounding pleased with himself.

"Yes, really clever," said Boff. "We wished we'd thought of it first."

"It's a trick!" whispered Doris. "Don't listen to him!"

"It's just that there's something really important," Boff went on. "It's not a joke, honestly. It's really serious."

"What?" Suspiciously.

"There was a buff folder there. On Mr Elliott's bed. I need it back. I've got to post it to my aunt."

"We didn't touch it," Cedric's voice came through the canvas.

"Look, it's really important. It's not mine, it belonged to Mrs Vormann. I need it back now, tonight."

"I told you," said Cedric, getting irritated. "We never touched it."

"Cedric...."

"We didn't take it," Doris interrupted. "We saw it, and we were going to take it, but we didn't. We saw it was Mrs Vormann's, that's why. Satisfied?"

"Are you sure?" Boff felt uneasy. He made a last appeal

107

to the one member of the Igmopong who couldn't tell a lie because he was too stupid. "Andy!"

A bloated voice materialised from the tent.

"What?"

"I want to hear you say it. Did any of you take the folder?"

"No," said Andy straight away. "We took the food, but we didn't take the folder thing. It was boring, anyway."

At last Boff was satisfied with their story, but his worry was redoubled. The folder had been there with the midnight feast when Charlotte and Jayne had left. If the Igmopong hadn't taken it, who had?

Deep in thought, they continued their journey to the Naitabal hut. Half an hour later, they were all dreaming of revenge.

"However did you think of doing the typewriting?" said Doris, still impressed. She was cramming another doughnut into her mouth, the jam was running down her chin, and she didn't care. "It was brilliant!"

"It even had *my* hair standing on end!" said Amanda.

"And mine," said Andy.

"We didn't know it was *you* doing it."

"We thought someone had really come in the back door, and really typed on the typewriter, and really gone out again," Doris went on, licking her lips and running a sticky finger up her chin.

"So did I," said Andy. "I heard him walk right past my cupboard, and he really *sounded* big and heavy, just like a real man would."

Cedric chuckled in the torchlight of the tent, enjoying himself. He didn't dare tell them that he had been just as frightened, and that none of it had been his doing at all. Instead, he cut another slice of Naitabal jelly, laid it between two thin pieces of bread, and took a huge bite. The raspberry-flavoured gel squirmed out at the sides and oozed down his cheeks.

"I thought that'd frighten 'em off," he mumbled. "I wish we could have seen their faces."

"They tried to press their buzzer thing for help," said Doris, chuckling. "I heard 'em. It was Charlotte and Jayne."

"They were scared," said Amanda. "Really scared."

The conversation went on in much the same vein until all the Naitabal food had disappeared, and one by one they fell asleep.

Cedric lay awake a little longer than the others. And suddenly, as he savoured each precious moment of the night's adventure, an idea came to him. A brilliant idea. An idea that would keep him as undisputed leader of his gang. It would make it look as though he really had master-minded the mysterious typing all along... But he couldn't tell the others. He'd have to arrange it secretly during tomorrow. Then they'd be even more impressed...

CHAPTER TWELVE

Assword-pong

"If Cedric didn't take it, who did?"

It was seven o'clock in the morning. Four Naitabals were breakfasting on a tin of assorted toffees and home-made sherbet water, and they were all asking the same question they had been asking themselves half the night. The fifth Naitabal, Toby, was still making snoring noises deep inside his sleeping-bag.

"It's got to be Mr Maynard," Charlotte said for the umpteenth time. "No one else knew Mrs Vormann's things had been moved to Mr Elliott's house."

"But why would *he* want it?" said Jayne.

"Why would *anyone* want it?" said Ben.

It was no use asking Toby's opinion.

"He's been acting suspiciously all along," Charlotte went on. "Touching his slimy hands on everything, and then wanting the desk for more than it was worth, and then wanting the typewriter for more than it was worth. And now wanting Mrs Vormann's book. That's not worth anything, probably."

Ben unwrapped a liquorice toffee and popped it into his mouth.

"That's funny," he said.

"What's funny?"

"They're all things to do with writing."

"What are?"

"All the things HMS *Slugface* wanted. Don't you see? The desk is something you write on, the typewriter's something you write on, and Mrs Vormann's book has been written?"

"Probably with the same typewriter on the same desk, as well," said Jayne.

Boff suddenly became more alert.

"You're right, Ben. And HMS *Slugface* is a writer, too."

"Except," Jayne reminded them, "he's never had any of his forty-nine books published. He must be a pretty rotten one."

"I don't know about anyone else," said Charlotte, "but I want to go to the loo. I'll be able to concentrate then."

The rope ladder was lowered, and Charlotte made her way through the Sea of Debris towards Mr Elliott's house. As she emerged from behind the skip, making for the road, a voice spoke behind her.

"Excuse me?"

Charlotte stopped and swivelled round. A young woman, dressed in a smart black suit and with a slim black briefcase in one hand, was stepping towards her from the direction of Mr Elliott's front door. She looked like the woman Ben had described from the evening before.

"Yes?"

"Do you live here?"

"No. This is Mr Elliott's house."

"Are you keeping an eye on it while he's away, then?"

"Sort of." Charlotte didn't want to say any more. This woman, pleasant as she seemed, was a stranger. Charlotte knew that people could act friendly just to find out things that were none of their business.

"Then I think I need to talk to you," the woman went on. "And the friend of yours I met yesterday."

"You're the solicitor, aren't you?"

"That's right. I see bad news travels fast."

Charlotte gave a cautious smile, then said daringly, "Do solicitors often work on Sundays?" and bit her lip and wished she hadn't thought of saying it.

Miss Gould laughed a silvery laugh.

"Not if they've any sense, they don't. But this case is rather important, and I need to talk to you – all of you."

"All of us?"

Miss Gould lowered her voice and fixed Charlotte with a knowing gaze.

"Well at least," she said, "all the ones who creep around houses at midnight."

Charlotte felt her cheeks warming up. She took a deep breath, then said, "I don't think we should talk to strangers," and started to walk on.

Miss Gould took a few steps forward.

"Would you like me to explain to your parents first?" she said quietly, " – so I'm not a stranger any more?"

Charlotte stopped again and turned. Despite her caution, she was dying to know what Miss Gould wanted with Mrs Vormann's things, and how she knew the Naitabals had been in Mr Elliott's house last night.

"All right," she said, and added hastily, "As long as you don't mention about creeping around houses at midnight."

"Okay."

Charlotte parked Miss Gould on her doorstep, leaving her there while she went to the toilet. Then she dragged her father away from his book and led him by one arm to the front door.

"I didn't hear the doorbell," Mr Maddison protested, bewildered. The thriller he was reading had reached an exciting part, and he wanted to get back to it. He didn't want boring everyday things to worry about on a Sunday.

"This lady wants to talk to you," said Charlotte.

"I'm Julie Gould," said the visitor, handing over a card. "Mr – ?"

"Maddison. Sorry. John Maddison. What can I do for you?"

"I'm a journalist, and I'm researching into Aspects of Play in the Modern Suburban Environment for a series of articles on the Modern Child..."

Charlotte's mouth dropped open as she looked from Miss Gould's innocent face to the card that Mr Maddison was holding that said:

JULIE GOULD

JOURNALIST

She was just about to protest when she caught a strange warning look in the corner of Miss Gould's eye.

Mr Maddison turned to Charlotte with a frown.

"Do you know what this is about? I don't understand all this modern child stuff..."

Charlotte nodded. "Yes. She wants to ask us some questions."

"Oh, I see," – to the visitor – "Why didn't you say so, then?"

"Sorry."

"It's just that Miss Gould is a stranger, Dad, and we don't talk to strangers, do we?"

"No, no, we don't," said Mr Maddison, suddenly remembering that they didn't. Then he smiled, anxious to get back to his book. "But now that Miss Gould has introduced herself, I'm sure she's fine. Perhaps you could just show me your driving licence as well, to make sure?"

Miss Gould delved into her wallet and produced the document, which Mr Maddison checked.

In the meantime, Charlotte had been working out what Miss Gould was up to. It wouldn't have been much use telling her father that she wanted to ask questions about Mrs Vormann's things, because he would have said it was none of her business and sent her packing. In the circumstances, Charlotte decided to take out an insurance policy of her own.

Looking Miss Gould straight in the eye, she said, "Miss Gould said you can keep her driving licence. She'll leave her car keys with you as well, Dad, just to make sure."

This time it was Miss Gould's turn to open and shut her mouth. She realised that Charlotte had got her own back.

"Yes," she said, still smiling. She produced the keys, dropped them into Mr Maddison's hand and pointed across the road to where the black sports coupé stood. "My driving licence and my car keys. So I can't run away."

Mr Maddison was impressed. The car was just the sort he'd always fancied for himself.

"Fair enough," he said, then turned to Charlotte. "But only answer general questions, mind," he warned. "Don't tell Miss Gould anything that we wouldn't want to see in the newspapers."

"No, Dad."

"And let us have a copy of the article when it's finished, eh?"

Without waiting for an answer, Mr Maddison escaped from boring reality, and stole back to the much more exciting world of heroes and villains in his book.

A few minutes later, Charlotte was steering Miss Gould down the obstacle-strewn path that wound to the Naitabal hut. They reached the huge oak tree with its branches arched above them like a giant umbrella, and Charlotte led them to one side, as far from the Igmopong Lightship as possible.

"Wait here," she said. "But I'm warning you – you might think getting past my father was easy—"

"It's already cost me my car," murmured Miss Gould.

" – but you'll need a password to get into the Naitabal hut."

"The Naitabal – ?" began Miss Gould. Then, "Oh, you mean the tree-house? What sort of a password?"

"That's up to you. Only three grown-ups have ever got in, and one of those was Mr Elliott because he built it and he can come in whenever he likes."

"A tough standard, obviously," murmured Miss Gould. "I really don't know what sort of password to give you."

114

"You said it was important?"

"Very important."

"How very important? A matter of life and death?"

"It could be."

Charlotte's eyes grew wider.

"You mean *really* life or death?"

"Yes." Then Miss Gould's face went very serious, and she added, "And that means I've just thought of a password."

The murmur of their voices drifted into the Naitabal hut through the trap-door, and Ben got up to look outside.

"Who is it?" said Boff.

"It's Charlotte. She's under the three-rope bridge, and she's with the lady I spoke to yesterday."

"What are they doing?"

"Talking. And pointing up here."

"I hope Charlotte doesn't invite her in without a jolly good reason," said Boff.

"She won't. Not Charlotte."

"We don't want just *any* grown-ups to share our secrets."

"The lady's getting a big envelope out of her briefcase," Ben's commentary continued. "And Charlotte's looking inside it... and her mouth has just dropped open... and she looks like one end of the Channel Tunnel."

"What?"

Boff and Jayne raised themselves to the window. It was true. Charlotte's face was as white as a flour-bomb. She had taken the envelope from the lady and was heading purposefully towards the rope ladder. She came up through the trap-door looking as if she'd seen the Ghost of Christmas Past.

"What is it?" said Boff.

"It's her password," said Charlotte.

Toby sensed that something important was happening and chose that moment to crawl half way out of his sleeping-bag.

115

"Is it morning yet?" he mumbled, but didn't get any answers.

Charlotte's hand was shaking with excitement as she held up the package.

"She wants to talk to us. She said it's a matter of life and death. I told her she'd need a password, and this is what she gave me." She held it out.

Boff took the bundle and pulled out the contents. It was a familiar buff folder.

"Mrs Vormann's book!" said Jayne. "She's found it!"

"I think we can ask her up now, don't you?" said Charlotte.

No one had any objections, and everyone agreed that it was the best password they could have had. Boff was relieved, but they were all wondering how Miss Gould could have got hold of it. Had Cedric given it to her? It was a question too intriguing to ignore.

"I suppose we'd better look tidy if she's coming up," said Toby. He extricated himself from his sleeping-bag and started a quick clearing-up operation.

Although Miss Gould was in a skirt and jacket, and carrying a briefcase, she ascended the rope ladder with a style that suggested she often spent Sunday mornings climbing rope ladders into tree-houses. Once inside, she looked round at the five expectant, fascinated faces and gave them all a disarming smile.

Ben and Charlotte hauled in the rope ladder and closed the trap-door. A small chair was provided for Miss Gould, and the others squeezed themselves into a tight semicircle against the opposite wall.

"I owe you an explanation," began Miss Gould, "and I expect you want to know what this matter of life and death is all about? First of all, though, I need to know what you children know."

"About what?" said Boff.

"About that." She pointed to the buff folder.

"Mrs Vormann's book?" said Jayne.

Their visitor looked up quickly.

"So you know what it is, then?"

"Of course," said Jayne, matter-of-fact. "It's got her name on it."

"Yes – but can you tell me *how much* you know about it?"

Boff was struggling to put together the right words of caution, but Ben said them first.

"Why should we?" he said. "We don't know anything about you. But we know that Mr Elliott is Mrs Vormann's executor, and it's up to him to make sure her things go to all the right places."

"That's right," said Boff. "That's what he told us, and we believe him."

"He wouldn't lie to us," said Jayne defiantly. "We're Naitabals."

"I see," said Miss Gould. "And, of course, you're quite right again. Why should you tell me anything?" She took a deep breath. "If I tell you a secret – I mean, a *real* secret – can you promise to keep it?"

"We're good at keeping secrets," said Charlotte. "We keep them all the time here, don't we?"

The others nodded.

"We know secrets about people that we'll never, never tell," said Ben.

"And secrets about us," said Jayne.

"Well," Miss Gould went on, "my secret is so important that you might be tempted to boast to your friends in school."

"We wouldn't," said Boff. "None of our secrets go outside the Naitabal hut."

"What about your friends in the tent next door?"

"*Friends*!" said everyone together. "Enemies, you mean!"

Miss Gould seemed satisfied.

"All right. The first thing I have to confess is that

117

yesterday I told you a little white lie. I'm afraid I'm *not* a solicitor." She sighed. "Sometimes I wish I were. The hours are easier, for one thing."

"But you had a card," said Ben.

"Yes," said Charlotte accusingly, "and she showed one to my father that said she was a journalist."

"Sorry. I'm not a journalist, either."

"Does that mean my Dad can keep your car, then?" – hopefully.

"No-o. But never trust a card. Anyone can get a card printed."

"What are you, then?"

"Actually, I work for the government. In a department called MI5 – the counter-espionage division of Military Intelligence."

There was a deathly hush, and five Naitabal jaws suddenly lost the use of their muscles and sagged open.

"Oh dear," smiled Miss Gould, "I can see all your fillings!"

The mouths closed again.

"That's the *first* thing you mustn't tell a living soul," she went on relentlessly, still smiling.

"What – about our fillings?" said Toby.

"No! Me being a member of MI5. And the second thing that you mustn't tell anyone – yet – is that Mrs Vormann, the lady of ninety-two who died recently, was for many years a member of MI6 – the espionage division of British Intelligence."

"You mean she was a *spy*?" said Ben. "I *said* she might be!"

"*Spy Quest*!" whispered Jayne, nudging Charlotte.

"Yes," said Miss Gould. "She was a spy. Of course, she hadn't been active for over thirty years, but MI5 always keeps an eye on ex-spies in case they try to write their memoirs. Our enquiries always suggested that she hadn't written any, or if she had, they were well hidden. She had knowledge of scores of people involved in Intelligence, you see, and it's always important that certain names should not be made public by publishing a book. It could put those people in great danger. That's why, when she died, we decided to make sure she hadn't written anything. If she had, any names in the book would have to be changed to fictitious ones before finding a publisher. That's why I need to find out what you children know about this." She indicated the buff folder.

"What makes you think we know anything?" said Ben.

Miss Gould settled her big blue eyes on him.

"Because," she said, "I was in Mr Elliott's house last night – around midnight. Is that good enough?"

"So you didn't *find* it, you *stole* it!"

"I'm afraid so. I had already done a thorough search of Mrs Vormann's house without success. Then I learned that some of her furniture had been moved to Mr Elliott's house, but my search of the furniture downstairs proved fruitless. After your 'friends' had gone and taken your midnight feast, I went upstairs. I was delighted to see a manuscript lying there on the bed, especially when I saw it had Mrs Vormann's name on it."

"Why have you brought it back, then?" asked Charlotte, asking the obvious, "after going to all that trouble to steal it?"

"The answer takes me back to my original question – what do you children – sorry, Naitabals – know about it?"

Jayne explained how she had found it in the secret drawer of the oak desk, and how Boff had carried it round half the evening, meaning to take it home and post it to his aunt.

"Mrs Vormann wrote to my aunt from the hospital before she died and told her where it was, and to find it if anything happened to her," added Boff.

"And is this what you found?" Miss Gould tapped the

folder and handed it across to the girls.

Charlotte flipped it open, and squealed.

"Jayne! Look!"

Jayne looked.

"What's the matter?"

Charlotte was holding out the top sheet.

"It's different!"

CHAPTER THIRTEEN

Ost-ming Ecret-song

"What do you mean, it's different?"

"Look! This wasn't done on that old Oliver typewriter! The typeface is different. The words are smaller! And the 'o's and the 'p's and the little 'e's aren't filled in! It's not the same manuscript we saw!"

"But how can it be different?" Jayne took the top sheet from her. It was true. Not only did it look different, but the first page didn't have the chapter heading.

"Don't you remember? The first page said '*Spy Quest* by Hermine Vormann', but it had 'Chapter One – The Death Papers', as well."

"Yes," said Jayne. "And the story started on the same page."

"But look at this. The chapter heading's on the next page, and it isn't called 'The Death Papers', it's called 'The Man in Munich'. It's completely different!"

The others had listened to the girls' exclamations in silence, but now Miss Gould spoke again.

"When I arrived home late last night and started reading it, I realised it wasn't the work of Hermine Vormann – well, certainly not her own life story, anyway – particularly as it's told in the first person by a man. It didn't have anything to do with the sort of spy Mrs Vormann was. So, Naitabals, what I want to know is: where's the original?"

"HMS *Slugface* has got it," said Ben, straight away.

"Dare I ask?" said Miss Gould. "HMS what? Who?"

"Sorry – Mr Maynard."

"Ah, yes. Slug face. Very appropriate."

"But how can it have been changed?" said Ben. "The one the girls found in the van was the right one. Then we found it again after we'd moved the desk, and Boff kept it with him all the time."

Boff pointed to the sheet Charlotte was holding.

"But that's the same one I saw," he said. "It must have been switched already."

"What happened in the van – exactly?" said Ben.

"I remember seeing Mr Maynard staring out of his bedroom window," said Charlotte. "That was the first thing. After that, Jayne started fiddling with the desk and we forgot all about him. Then Jayne found the manuscript, and we heard Mr Maynard coming out of his gate. He must have been watching us, but I'm sure Jayne got the secret drawer back before he came close enough to see anything."

"And after that?"

Charlotte's face wrinkled as if she had found Mr Maynard in her lettuce.

"He started putting his slimy mitts all over everything, and his beady eyes, and starting offering Mr Elliott lots of money for the desk."

Boff's eyes had narrowed, and he was staring at Jayne.

"Did you leave him alone with the desk?"

"No. He went back home to get changed, and we—" Jayne stopped. "Oh dear... We went into the house to have a drink. We played with the typewriter and cleaned the ink out of the messy letters, and..." Her voice trailed off.

"And Mr Maynard was a long time changing," Boff finished for her. "Long enough for him to find the secret drawer and do the switch..."

"And if anyone had caught him, he'd've said he was just looking at the desk..." murmured Miss Gould.

"But why would *he* want to steal her book?" said Charlotte. "Is he a spy as well?"

"Oh, no," said Miss Gould. "No, certainly not."

Then Boff latched on, and began to look excited.

"Of course!" he said. "That's it!"

"What's what?"

"That's the answer! HMS *Slugface* is a writer, and he's been trying to get his own books published for years! His next door neighbour – a sweet old lady of ninety-two – tells him she's written a book, but she doesn't want it published until after she dies."

"No," said Miss Gould, shaking her head. "She wouldn't have told him. It was far too secret for that. He might have seen it by accident somehow..."

"Well, he reads it, and he realises it's brilliant, and when she dies he wants to get hold of it so that he..." Boff's voice disappeared as the full realisation came to him.

"So he what?" said Jayne.

"So he can get it published under his own name!"

"You mean pretend he wrote it himself?"

"Of course! What else?"

Suddenly disappointment hung in the air.

"That was yesterday morning," said Ben. "He'll have posted it off to a publisher by now."

But Miss Gould had realised something as well. She leaned forward, full of excitement.

"No! No, he won't! Not yet!"

"Why? How can you know?"

"Because of what happened in Mr Elliott's house last night..."

"What do you mean?"

"Listen. This all fits. Everything fits, and it's very clever of Boff to work it out."

"What fits, Miss Gould? Please tell us."

"I was there in Mr Elliott's house last night, as I've already said. I used skeleton keys to get in the front door, and I started looking through the drawers of Mrs Vormann's desk to find the manuscript. Then you girls arrived and I hid behind the door. You hadn't been there long when I heard a key turn in the back door. I stayed in the shadows. A man came in – a man with a bald head and rounded shoulders. I recognised him. It was Mrs Vormann's next-door neighbour, Mr Maynard."

The Naitabals held their breath.

"He took out a sheet of paper and laid it on the desk. He put a blank piece of paper into the typewriter, and started typing. It didn't occur to me that he was doing anything connected with Mrs Vormann. I didn't want to give myself away, so I kept quiet."

"Do you mean," said Charlotte, trying to make it clear, "that it was Mr Maynard doing the typing, and not Cedric?"

"Cedric?"

Charlotte pointed to the tent next door.

"Oh, no. Cedric didn't do anything. When Mr Maynard had finished typing, and you two girls had gone for help, Cedric and his friends just crawled out of the furniture like woodworm. They must have been there all the time. Then they helped themselves to your midnight feast."

"The beasts!"

"When it seemed the house was empty of all this human traffic, I carried on searching the desk, but in vain. So I went upstairs. And there it was, lying on the bed. I didn't know it at the time, but it had been switched, of course."

"But what I don't understand," said Ben, "is why Mr Maynard went in and used the old typewriter?"

"Simple!" said Miss Gould. "*He had to re-type the first page with his own name on it*! He must have thought it safer to use the original typewriter Mrs Vormann had used. Someone reading it might have thought it rather odd to have the title page, with the author's name, typed on a different typewriter. If he didn't do that, he would have had to re-type the whole five hundred pages on his own typewriter! And he's far too impatient for that!"

124

"So that's why he wanted the typewriter as well as the desk!" said Charlotte.

"In the end he didn't need the desk, because he'd already switched the book!" said Jayne.

"And when he didn't get the typewriter," Charlotte finished, "he decided to borrow it instead! Last night!"

"And that," concluded Miss Gould, "is how I know he hasn't posted it to the publishers yet!"

"How do you know that?" said Jayne.

"Well, he couldn't have posted it yesterday because he only had a complete manuscript this morning. And he can't post it today because it's Sunday!"

"Of course he can," said Toby, yawning. "All he's got to do is stick it in the post box."

Miss Gould held up the buff folder.

"This is too big to go into a post box!" she said. "He'll have to wait until tomorrow morning, when the post office is open!"

At last light dawned in the Naitabal consciousness, and there were sighs of relief all round.

"So that means we've got until tomorrow morning to get the manuscript back?" said Boff.

"Yes," said Miss Gould. "That's it precisely."

The Naitabals felt happy that at last the strange behaviour of HMS *Slugface* was explained. But what next?

"I'm afraid it does mean another substitution," Miss Gould continued.

"But how do we know," said Boff slowly to Miss Gould, "that you're who you say you are? You might be a *double* spy working for a foreign enemy..."

"Oh dear," sighed Miss Gould, and her face went very serious-looking. She turned and spoke to the thick oak branch that rose diagonally through the tree-house. "Why are modern children so *bright*? Why can't they believe everything they're told by strangers the way children used to,

125

and get themselves into lots of trouble?"

Before anyone had time to comment, Miss Gould's face broke into a mischievous smile.

"Oh, if you could see your faces!" she said.

None of the Naitabals quite knew what was going on, and they looked to Boff and Ben for some sort of lead.

"That's the trouble with spies, isn't it?" said Ben at last. "You never know who's on your side?"

Miss Gould shook her head solemnly.

"I'm afraid you don't."

"So we need another password, don't we?" said Charlotte. "Something to prove you're really on our side?"

"Yes. Yes, I suppose you do. But of course, there's nothing to stop me breaking into Mr Maynard's house tonight and getting the book without your help, is there?"

"Yes, there is," said Ben. "If you don't give us a new password right now – even better than the first one – we'll have to tell Mr Maynard we know he took the manuscript and that spies are trying to pinch it. Then we could hide it where you'd *never* find it."

"*Roject-pong Ubmarine-song*," whispered Jayne.

Miss Gould tried to catch what Jayne had said, but didn't have a chance with such a quiet voice, and with no knowledge of Naitabal language. The twinkle was still in her eye as she said: "If I was really your enemy, I'd go to Mr Maynard's house now, threaten him with prosecution, and make him hand it over. You wouldn't have a chance to warn him."

"We could get to Mr Maynard's house quicker than you could," boasted Ben, thinking of the raid on Mr Maynard's pear tree the previous morning. "Because we don't have to bother with boring things like human roads."

Miss Gould was still smiling at them, as much intrigued by their conversation as they were by hers.

"Perhaps one of us had better go now," said Boff.

"Jayne was quickest," said Ben. "She can go."

"Oh, thanks," said Jayne, getting up. "You're not taking much of a chance, are you?"

"Shouldn't have been quickest, should you?"

"All right, all right," said Miss Gould, holding up two hands in surrender. "I am on your side, honestly! I'll think of another password!"

There was a silence. Five Naitabals watched as their visitor struggled to think of something convincing. She still hadn't come up with anything when Ben spoke again.

"Why can't we all go to Mr Maynard now? Tell him we know he's pinched the book, and make him hand it over?"

"Because it's boring," said Charlotte.

"Yes," said Toby, beginning to come alive. "He tricked us out of it, so we should trick him back."

"It'll be much more fun," said Jayne, clasping her hands together.

No one disagreed that it would be much more fun, but Boff put in his usual steadying word.

"The only way to get it back now," he said, "is to go into his house when he's not there – or tonight when he's asleep – and take it. And that could be dangerous."

"Yes, but it's fun," said Charlotte, agreeing with Jayne. "What's the point of being Naitabals if we don't do things the exciting way?"

Boff was still convinced that it was too risky, and without a unanimous Naitabal decision, nothing could happen. Miss Gould had been very quiet, thinking and listening, but now she spoke again.

"I'm going to show you something," she said. "But the only reason I'm showing it to you is because I don't want you rushing to Mr Maynard and spilling the beans. This is *absolutely top secret*, so I need another promise from you all."

Five Naitabals promised never, ever to tell anyone

anything.

Miss Gould laid her briefcase flat on her knees and tapped eight digits into the keypad on its front. There was a click and the lid opened.

"Isn't it a bit risky carrying all these top secret things around in your briefcase?" said Boff. "What if the enemy gets hold of it?"

"Well, first they need the code to open it. If they get the code wrong twice, or if they try to break the case open, the contents will self-destruct."

"You mean it blows up?" said Ben.

"Not exactly. But everything inside gets vaporised." Miss Gould delved into it and extracted a flimsy sheet of shiny paper. "This is the fax I received from MI5 yesterday," she went on. "And, of course, it's my second password."

It was headed "MOST SECRET".

"Do they send 'most secret' things down the telephone line?" said Jayne, surprised.

"Don't worry," smiled Miss Gould. "It's sent in code. I have a device that plugs into my telephone line to unscramble it when it reaches my fax machine. That way, no one else on the line can make any sense of it."

"A bit like Naitabal language, then," said Charlotte.

"And Naitabal letters," said Jayne.

"We'll have to teach Miss Gould how to write a Naitabal letter," said Ben. "Then she can write to us in code as well."

They read the fax. It said:

> Following the death of Hermine Vormann, British agent 4474, imperative any autobiography written by same be recovered immediately for removal of names identifying other British agents still active.

There followed a whole page of typing, including Mrs Vormann's address and other personal details.

"Is that good enough, Naitabals?" she said.

Five heads nodded simultaneously.

"Good. Let's make plans for tonight, then." Miss Gould's eyes laughed. "It's a good job Naitabals like lurking in dark houses, isn't it?"

CHAPTER FOURTEEN

The Great Chair Hunt

A Naitabal whistle, loud and shrill, invaded the peaceful Sunday morning of Naitabal territory. It penetrated the triple glazing in the doctor's house on Corner Island and woke him from a pleasant dream. It pierced the kitchen wall of Ben's house, making Mr Tuffin bang his head on the waste pipe he was fixing. It travelled down Miss Coates's chimney and frightened the cat that was dozing on the hearthrug. It rattled the wine glasses on Mr Maynard's dresser and made him jump from his seat in the study. And it ripped through two layers of Igmopong canvas like a tidal wave, making the occupants sit up in their sleeping-bags, thinking the world was coming to an end.

Toby, the perpetrator of the whistle, inhaled deeply to get his breath back and turned, satisfied, to Jayne.

"That's how you do it," he said.

Jayne removed her hands from her ears.

"But you didn't use your fingers," she said. "Most people stick two fingers in the sides of their mouth."

"It's not a Naitabal whistle if you use any fingers," said Toby. "Look. You tighten your lower lip against your bottom teeth..."

Jayne tried to copy as Toby demonstrated.

"Then you rest the tip of your tongue just behind it..."

"'Ike 'iss?" said Jayne, indistinctly.

"That's it. Then moisten your top lip, bring down your top teeth – and *blow*!"

Jayne and the others covered their ears as Toby let rip with another blast that would have done credit to a steam

130

locomotive. Anyone in the Naitabal domain who might have fancied a nice Sunday morning lie-in was rudely disappointed.

"Wow!" said Jayne, impressed. "Can you all do that?"

"Yes," said Charlotte. She demonstrated with a more modest shrill. "But Toby's the best."

Jayne tried and tried, but could only get a noise that sounded like air hissing out of a fatally wounded balloon.

"Keep trying," Charlotte encouraged her. "None of us could do it at first – only Toby."

Miss Gould had long gone, and the Naitabals were preparing for the great Challenge with the Igmopong.

"We'll need the Naitabal whistle," Charlotte went on, "to call each other in the woods when we spread out."

The others nodded as Jayne struggled to produce a note.

"And Naitabal battledress, of course," said Ben. "I'll get it." He leaned down, opened the little cupboard door beneath the diagonal branch, and started pulling out pieces of clothing and equipment. Then he and Charlotte sorted out which were whose, and checked them off item by item.

"Naitabal headbands lined with emergency supply of red liquorice rope," said Charlotte.

"Check," said Ben.

"Peashooter and dried peas. Peashooter to double as Naitabal flute when in need of urgent clarion call."

"Yep."

"Survival kit in case of capture by Igmopong."

"Check."

"Including matchbox containing survival food – sultanas, chopped dates, broken raw spaghetti, jelly cake decorations, nuts, and emergency energy pill (glucose)."

"All present."

"Bribery kit (mostly cash) for bribing captors in kidnap situation."

"Check. Or should I say Cheque?"

"Very funny," said Toby.

"Pencil, paper, envelope and small denomination stamps for Naitabal letter and envelope coding."

"Yep."

"Water-bottle for drinking or throwing, including supply of ready-folded paper water-bomb cases for filling."

"Uh-huh."

"First aid kit including safety pin, aspirin, plasters and cotton wool."

"All present."

"And we need to collect bows, arrow quivers, torches, Swiss knives, chocolate rations, rope and string."

"That's it. All present, then."

Jayne still hadn't managed to produce a whistle, but her imitation of a dying balloon had now veered towards wind howling in a sewage pipe.

"That means you're getting better," said Toby.

Presently, there were visible signs of the Igmopong stirring on Pigmo Island. Toby despatched a message by arrow for a rendezvous in half an hour, and then everyone was ready to don Naitabal battledress.

Gray's Wood bordered the whole of the western side of the Straits of Brunswick, and was half a mile deep. Two strange-looking groups stood at the entrance to the public footpath opposite Mr Elliott's house. One group surrounded a brightly-painted red chair, and the other a bright yellow one.

As well as being separated by mutual distrust, the Naitabals and the Igmopong were so many metres apart that they had to raise their voices to speak to each other. Normally, the Igmopong felt the comfort and protection of a garden fence between themselves and the Naitabals, and could hurl insults in comparative safety. But now, every time the Naitabals took a step forward to avoid shouting, the

Igmopong took two steps back.

Cedric's gang were specially frightened of reprisals for their excesses of the night before. Nevertheless, Cedric's face still managed to wear a confident smirk, as if he had had a personal message from God that he couldn't possibly lose.

"So what's this challenge, then?" said Doris, who didn't need to raise her normal voice to be heard. "And it had better be fair, otherwise it won't count."

"Oh, it's fair all right," called Ben. As it was mostly his idea, he was acting as organiser. "It's a treasure hunt."

"What's the treasure?" She said it so loud and so quickly, that Cedric had no chance of getting a word in sideways.

"You're looking at it," said Ben. "A red chair and a yellow chair."

"Don't think much of that," moaned Doris. "Not what I call treasure."

"All right, we'll call it the Great Chair Hunt, then."

"That's better. What do we have to do?"

"If you'll just let *me* explain –" began Cedric, but was rudely interrupted by Doris.

"Shut up. I'm listening to Ben Tuffin."

"You chose red, didn't you?" said Ben to Cedric.

"Yes," – hastily – "because *yellow* suits *you* better!"

"Now, now, Cedric. That was my line, not yours. Anyway, you hide your red chair in the woods, and we hide the yellow chair. Then you all try to find our yellow chair, and we try to find your red chair. And the ones who bring the others' chair back to Mr Elliott's front garden first, are the winners."

"You mean," said Cedric, "if we bring your yellow chair back first, we have your tree-house for a week, and if you bring our red chair back first, you have my boat for a week?"

"That's it."

"It's stupid," boomed Doris. "We'll just follow you and watch where you put yours, and then you'll sneak up on us

133

and watch where we put ours."

"No you won't. Because one of each gang will stay behind with the other gang to make sure there's no cheating."

"What do you mean?" said Amanda.

"Yeah..." said Andy. "What'd'you mean?"

"When we go and hide the yellow chair, Boff will stay here with you four to make sure you don't follow. When we get back, three of you go and hide the red chair, and one of you stays with us to make sure—"

"Okay, we get it, we get it," interrupted Doris impatiently. "But what's to stop us burying it? You'd never find it if we buried it."

"Here are the other rules," said Ben. He took a step forward, holding out a sheet of paper. The Igmopong tripped up each other's feet as they retreated nervously. "Come on, one of you. I've written them down. Then no one can say afterwards they didn't know the rules."

Cedric shoved Andy in the small of the back, propelling him towards Ben. The sheet was snatched and Andy scurried back with it. They read:

1. Chair must be hidden in Gray's Wood.
2. No more than 20 minutes to hide chair.
3. No burying the chair in earth/soil etc, but bushes okay.
4. You can use any material, ropes, etc, to help hide it (refer Mr Elliott's garden).
5. Winners are ones who *bring back* the rivals' chair first.
6. Winners must show losers where their chair was hidden to prove no cheating.
7. Any cheating loses the Challenge.

"Any questions?" said Ben.

The Igmopong went into a huddle, and several sniggers

emerged.

"No questions," said Cedric. "Who's going to hide their chair first?"

"You can, if you want."

"No," smirked Cedric. "You go first."

Ben nodded to Boff.

"We'll be back in under twenty minutes," he said. "Make sure your watches are synchronised."

Boff joined the Igmopong, watches were set, and the command of "Go!" was given. The four Naitabals, in full battledress, bows and arrows and coils of light rope slung round their shoulders, and a yellow chair swinging between them, ran up into the woods and disappeared from view.

"This one'll do," said Ben.

They were three breathless minutes into the wood, and Ben was pointing up at a tall, tall tree that stretched way up into the canopy.

"It's got a good branch on this side, see?"

Charlotte readied her bow and a single arrow, and they tied a length of thin thread to its shaft. Toby spun the rest of the thread out on to the ground in wide circles. Charlotte took careful aim and fired. The arrow soared over the branch in a beautiful, perfect arc, and the thread snaked up from the ground, following it.

"Did it!" she shouted, delighted with herself.

"Well done!" said Jayne.

Seconds later, Jayne was tying the end of a coil of rope to the thread, and minutes after that, Toby had tied the rope to the back of the chair. When everyone was happy it wouldn't fall off, they hoisted it up the tree.

They stood, necks craned up towards the sky, watching the yellow chair swinging gently to and fro.

"Just like yesterday!" said Jayne. "Another crow's nest!"

"I don't think I'd like to go up in that one, either," said

Ben.

"Now comes the tricky bit," said Toby.

With the arrow still attached to the thread, Charlotte fired it over a branch of the next tree along. Twice she missed, and twice they had to haul the thread back again, but it was third time lucky. Then the rope was hauled up once more so that it hung in a festoon from one branch to another. Charlotte fired into the canopy for the last time so that the arrow, the thread, the rope, and the chair were completely out of reach.

"They might *find* it," said Ben, laughing. "But they'll never bring it back!"

"And we haven't broken any of the rules!" said Jayne.

They all held each other's arms, facing in a circle heads down, and did a little war-dance. Then Charlotte looked at her watch.

"Six minutes to get back," she said, and they ran.

Boff and the Igmopong were sitting on Mr Elliott's front wall when Ben, Toby, Charlotte and Jayne returned with two minutes to spare. The Igmopong, apparently not needing ropes or other equipment, disappeared into the wood, leaving Andy to keep an eye on the Naitabals. Ten minutes later, Cedric, Doris and Amanda reappeared, minus the red chair, looking pleased with themselves.

"We were quicker'n you," said Cedric. "We've hidden ours where you'll *never* get it."

"So have we," said Charlotte.

Andy rejoined the Igmopong, and the two teams regrouped at a safe distance from each other.

"So the first one back here with the other's chair is the winner, right?" said Cedric.

"That's it."

"So if we're back here first with the yellow chair, we get your tree-house for a week?"

"Yes. And if we're back here first with the red chair, we

136

get your rubber boat for a week. Okay?"

"Yes," grinned Cedric. "When do we start?"

"Now," said Ben. "No point in wasting any time. You can go first, if you like."

"All right."

The Igmopong sidled towards the entrance to the wood, and slowly receded into its depths.

The Naitabals then set off at a run and spread out, but Jayne stayed with Toby because she couldn't do a Naitabal whistle yet.

Only ten minutes later, the deep woods reverberated with the piercing shrill of a double Naitabal whistle, which meant that one of them had found the red chair. The whistle was repeated, and was followed by the sound of Naitabal feet trampling the undergrowth as they homed in on the find.

Ben had found it. The chair had been thrown into the top of a wicked clump of brambles that was fully five metres across and twice as high as themselves. There was no way of retrieving it by hand unless one of them was willing to get badly scratched.

"We need a ladder, so we can crawl across and get it," said Ben, when all the others had arrived.

"Or a big hook on the end of a piece of rope," said Toby.

"We've got the rope, but we haven't got a hook," said Boff, thinking.

"What about a lasso?" suggested Charlotte.

"Brilliant!"

Another length of rope was uncoiled from a Naitabal shoulder, a slip knot was tied to make a running loop, and a few minutes later the lasso was ready. Jayne fancied herself as a cowgirl and made the first throw to try and get the loop over the chair. She twirled it over her head, threw it, and missed.

Then they took it in turns. After half a dozen throws, it was Jayne who finally did it. She pulled the loop tight round the chair, then pulled. It bounced across the huge bramble mound, and had to be dragged hard in places to free it from the clutching briars, waving like wild arms, that tried to pull it down. Carefully, they hauled in their prize.

By the time they returned, hot, tired, and feeling triumphant, they had been away for just twenty minutes.

But there, in Mr Elliott's front garden, stood the Igmopong. They were jeering and cat-calling and saying rude words, and Cedric was sitting like a king on the yellow chair.

CHAPTER FIFTEEN

Ost-gheng

The Naitabals stopped dead in their tracks. The red chair, borne from the woods and triumphantly held aloft, sagged slowly to the ground along with its bearers, Jayne and Charlotte.

"We've got your tree-house for a whole week!" chanted Cedric, laughing so much he almost fell off the chair. "A whole week, and nothing you can do about it!"

Doris's normally petulant face was now wearing a supercilious, and repulsive, smirk.

"Think you're so clever, don't you!" she taunted.

"That's impossible!" said Ben and Toby together, and Boff was just looking grim.

"You thought hoisting it up a tree was going to cause us big trouble, didn't you!" Cedric went on. "But it didn't! Getting it down was easy, easy, easy, peasy, peasy, peasy with our secret weapon, so don't think you're so clever, clever, clever in future, will you?"

"We couldn't have got it down ourselves in less than half an hour," Jayne whined to Charlotte, as they lay in a heap on the grassy bank of the wood. "And that would have needed a lot of luck."

"I don't know how they did it," Charlotte whimpered back, "but they have."

"I was looking forward to a week in Cedric's boat, as well."

Doris moved towards them and held out a grubby, freckled hand.

"We'll have the key of the tree-house now," she said.

"We didn't say you'd get it immediately," said Ben, and a great roar of derision went up from across the Straits of Brunswick.

"Ooh! Trying to wriggle out of it, now!"

"You cheats!"

"You *said*!"

"Yeah!"

"You can have it at ten o'clock tomorrow morning," Ben went on, feeling hot around his ears. "That'll give us time to clear our things out and have the midnight feast you robbed us of last night."

The howls of protest died down as a feeling of guilt mixed with ecstasy swept over the Igmopong.

"We didn't realise it was *your* midnight feast," oozed Cedric, sarcastically. "If we'd realised it was *yours*, we'd have left it alone. *Naturally*."

"We thought Mr Elliott had left it behind," Doris joined in. "We thought it might *spoil* if it was left for two or three weeks."

"How did you get in, anyway?" demanded Boff. "You'd no business to be in there in the first place."

"Wouldn't you like to know?"

"Yeah," said Andy. "Wouldn't you?"

"All I can tell you," Cedric went on jeeringly, "is that it was easy, easy, easy, peasy, peasy—"

"Oh, shut up!" said Charlotte and Jayne together, climbing to their feet.

The Naitabals came down off the woody bank and moved across the road to collect the yellow chair. The Igmopong scattered in panic.

"We're having a midnight feast tonight," taunted Cedric, from the safe distance of his garden gate. "But *we* won't be leaving it unguarded. And if you come anywhere *near* the tent, we'll—"

"You'll scream like little babies," Ben finished for him.

"We know."

Not for the first time in their lives, a great black cloud of misery had settled over the Naitabals' tree-house.

"Shall Jayne and I have another try at sleeping in Mr Elliott's house tonight?" said Charlotte, without much enthusiasm. "We might as well make the most of the tree-house excuse before we lose it."

"I suppose so," said Boff gloomily. "It's better than doing nothing. That reminds me – I've got to fix the alarm."

"Isn't there a way for us to know if it's working when we press it?" asked Jayne. "If there is, I'm sure you can think of it."

"I should have done it in the first place," said Boff, "but I didn't think of it being sabotaged."

"What can you do?"

"Put a torch bulb at each end, connected to the buzzer at the other end. If you press your button, and the bulb lights, it means the buzzer's working at our end."

"What if they cut the wire?"

"At least you'll know it's been cut. The bulb won't light if it's not connected to the batteries." Boff pointed to where they were mounted on the wall of the Naitabal hut, next to the buzzer.

"That sounds all right, then," said Jayne.

Ben emerged from a depressed silence.

"When Boff's done that, we've got to think of a way of getting even with the Igmopong," he said.

"I thought we'd get even with the treasure hunt," said Charlotte listlessly. "Having Cedric's blow-up boat for a week would have made up for everything."

"They've beaten us all the way," said Toby. "They had our midnight feast, and now they've got the Naitabal hut for a week."

"I still don't know how they did it," said Ben. "It's

impossible – at least, it's impossible when they've only got one brain cell between them."

"And that one's dying," said Toby.

"Well, we could bolt the back door of Mr Elliott's house tonight," said Ben. "They wouldn't be able to sneak in again and spoil things."

"We don't know if that's how they got in," said Charlotte. "And why should they try again? They've already spoilt things. They wouldn't do it again. They wouldn't dare."

"We should leave it *un*bolted and catch them if they come in again," suggested Jayne. She bunched her neat little fists. "And give 'em a good fight."

"Now, now, let's not get physical," said Boff. "No violence."

"Boff's right," said Ben. "We've got to out-smart them. Otherwise, we're no better than they are."

"And so far," concluded Toby gloomily, "they're looking like they've out-smarted us."

"It doesn't *look* like it," said Charlotte, equally miserable. "They have."

Then everyone looked outside as Harry came bouncing down the Sea of Debris and stopped underneath the Naitabal oak.

"Breakfastbang!" he announced in a loud and tuneless voice. "Eggsbang, baconbang and bangersbang!"

Charlotte, already in a bad mood, hurtled down the rope ladder and caught her brother by the arm before he had a chance to run off. She pulled his face close to hers.

"*Reakfast-bang, eggs-eng, acon-bang* and *angers-bang*!" she said, shaking him. As she shook him, she noticed something suspicious sticking out of his trouser pocket. "What's that?" she demanded.

Before he could look or answer, she grabbed it. It was an envelope that had been folded in half, and was showing bad signs of having travelled with Harry for a whole day.

142

"It's the letter for Mr Maynard!" she screamed, and shook him some more. "Harry! I told you to take this yesterday!"

"C-o-u-l-d-n-'t f-i-n-d t-h-e h-o-u-s-e," said Harry, rattling from the force of his sister's grip. "G-o-n-e-b-a-n-g!"

"What d'you mean, you couldn't find it? I told you it was next to Ben's house."

"You said Toby's house."

"No, I didn't."

"You did."

"Didn't."

"Did."

"Didn't."

"Didbang."

"Didn'tbang. There! You've got me saying it now!" Charlotte let out an exasperated lungful of air, and gave up. "We'll take it after breakfast," she said. "Come on."

All Sunday afternoon, the Sea of Debris sweltered in the Doldrums. There was no wind to stir the leaves of the Naitabal oak, and the naked sun beat down, warming the heaps of wood and rubbish, and the five sleeping-bags that hung on a line of rope. Pigmo Island was deserted, with no quarrelsome Igmopong voices polluting the air. Only the sounds of distant lawnmowers gave a clue to any human habitation.

But out of sight, in secret places, plans were being laid. A lady in black moved like a shadow through Mr Elliott's front garden, and joined a group of five children huddled inside the house. One of them had made a discovery: a window that led into the cellar. They talked in whispers, exchanging secrets. Next door, a group of four children lay on a bedroom floor, heads together, bodies stretched at right angles in the form of a cross, sucking pencils, writing on scraps of paper, talking in hushed voices, giggling. Not many houses away, a bald-headed man danced in circles in

143

his study. A ripped-open envelope lay on the floor, he was hugging a sheet of paper to his chest, and he was singing.

"What's HMS *Slugface* doing now?" said Boff.
"You wouldn't believe me if I told you," said Ben.
"I would."
"You wouldn't."
"Try me."

It was twenty minutes to midnight, and Ben was at the south window of the Naitabal hut once more, looking through the binoculars.

"He's got a paper hat on, he's dancing round in circles, he's conducting an imaginary orchestra, and he's singing."

"Oh, yes," said Boff. "He was doing all that earlier. He wasn't wearing a paper hat, though. That's new."

"I think he's mad. Do you think he's mad, Miss Gould?"

The lady from MI5 smiled in the darkness.

"He certainly seems to go from one extreme to the other. You told me he was motionless for hours on end, and now he's dancing for hours on end. Possible signs of a troubled mind, yes. It's obviously no use my paying him a visit for quite a while. I shall enjoy your invitation to the midnight feast instead. I haven't had a midnight feast for years."

"I wonder if Toby's all right?" said Boff. He was peering through the west window towards Pigmo Island, but apart from the suspicious, static glow coming from Cedric Morgan's tent, there was little to be seen other than silhouettes of trees and houses on the horizon.

"I'm sure he'll be fine," said Miss Gould. "It was clever of him to find it. You all did your preparations well. It's just a matter of timing now, and a bit of luck."

They all jumped as the buzzer on the wall suddenly sprang into life.

"Good!" said Boff. "That's the test. One buzz for testing, two for help, three for emergency help, and four to call the police. One buzz means Jayne and Charlotte are starting to get the feast ready."

Miss Gould was standing next to the buzzer.

"Shall I respond?"

"Yes, please. Just one, of course."

Miss Gould pressed the button. There was no sound this time, but the torch bulb that Boff had fitted glowed and faded.

"I do hope Toby remembered to take a screwdriver," said Miss Gould.

"Yes, he did," said Boff. "I saw him."

"And I hope he doesn't get cold, and I hope he doesn't go to sleep."

"Toby's nocturnal," said Ben. "He only sleeps in the morning."

A few more minutes passed, and then they all jumped again as the buzzer sounded for the second time.

"One buzz," said Boff aloud. "Two – there! The midnight feast is ready! *Three?!* Oh, no! It's emergency help! Come on!"

Ben and Miss Gould went down the rope ladder, leaving Boff to lock up and go out through the roof. As they made their way up the dark Sea of Debris, feeling with their feet for obstacles, they heard the creaks as Boff crossed the three-rope bridge to Boff Island.

It had been agreed that Boff would go to the front door with the key, while Miss Gould and Ben would get in via the back door, which they'd decided to leave unbolted. As the two of them neared the back of the house, Ben's foot tripped on something, there was a noisy clatter, and he stumbled forward.

"Ouch!" he cursed, but he wasn't really hurt. He felt stupid for making a noise at such a critical moment. Then he realised. It was a paint tin. He'd left them near the back door instead of putting them back where he'd found them, and it served him right for being lazy. As he rubbed his foot he heard Miss Gould's skeleton key turning in the back door lock, and he took two hurried steps to catch up with her in the gloom as the door swung inwards.

At a quarter to midnight, Charlotte pressed the button on the buzzer board in Mr Elliott's bedroom, and the torch bulb that Boff had fitted glowed and faded.

"One press for *testing*," chanted Jayne, who was next to her, holding a torch in the darkness. "Two for *come*, three for *help*, and four for *call the police*."

Seconds later, their own buzzer sounded once.

"Good," said Charlotte. "That means their buzzer worked, and they've tested ours."

For the second time in twenty-four hours, they opened a big cardboard box and started taking out food for their midnight feast.

"Jelly sandwiches," said Charlotte, "made up ready."

Jayne found the labels they had prepared, threaded them on to cocktail sticks, and pushed them in as Charlotte announced each item of fare.

"Slugs on Toast. Black jelly babies really, of course, but we'll tell the boys they're slugs."

"They look like slugs, the way they've melted," said Jayne.

"Cherryade to drink."

"That's Bat's Blood."

"Elderberry Crush," said Charlotte.

"Right."

"Dandelion and daisy leaf sandwiches."

"Good. I bet Miss Gould won't eat those."

"I bet she does. They're trained to survive in the wild."

"What's next?"

"Mouse pies."

"Oh, yes. Those tails sticking out the sides look really good. And the ears in the middle, as well."

146

"Thanks. Worm cast biscuits."

"I don't think *I'll* have any of those. They're too realistic."

They continued to unpack the box, whispering in the near-darkness.

At ten minutes to twelve, they both heard a noise. It wasn't the sound of a key in the front door, or of a key in the back door, but it was a noise they had heard before. It came from downstairs, and it was the old, unmistakable tapping of the typewriter.

"Tap-tap, tap-tap-tap, tap-tap, ting!"

"Here we go again!" whispered Jayne, more irritated than worried.

"I didn't hear anyone come," Charlotte whispered back, unconcerned. "And what's he typing now? We thought he'd done all that?"

The girls were used to the idea of disturbances by now, and hadn't even bothered to switch off their torches. Calmly, Charlotte reached across and pressed the help button once, twice, three times. The bulb glowed once, twice, three times, and they both felt safe and secure.

"What shall we do now?" whispered Jayne. "Go and look, or wait for the others?"

"Let's go and look. We know the others'll be here in minutes. And Miss Gould's with them."

"I wonder if Toby's back yet?"

"Come on."

"Tap, tap, tap, tap-tap, tap-tap-tap, tap, tap, ting!"

As carefully as they could, they crept down the stairs.

"Tap, tap-tap, tap!"

The door of the front room was closed. Charlotte stood next to it, hand poised on the doorknob, while Jayne pressed in close beside her. Suddenly, there was a clattering noise outside the back of the house, and moments later they heard keys being turned in front and back doors simultaneously. Charlotte took a deep breath and, even as Boff and Ben and

Miss Gould moved in silently behind her, the sound of typing stopped abruptly, as suddenly as it had begun. She threw open the door.

Five torches scanned the oak desk. A piece of paper in the old Oliver typewriter fluttered in the moving air.

But there was no one there.

CHAPTER SIXTEEN

Eats-chang Ever-ning Rosper-pong

"What happened?" said Ben.

"We heard the typing again," said Charlotte, mystified. "It only stopped two seconds ago. Didn't you hear it?"

"But there's no one there."

"There must have been."

"He couldn't have hidden in two seconds. Look. The furniture's too piled up."

Miss Gould put a hand on Charlotte's arm, and nodded towards behind the door – the place where she had hidden herself the previous night. Charlotte moved backwards and let Miss Gould squeeze through. Miss Gould walked into the room, then spun round with her torch. Her face showed disappointment.

"No one there, either," she said.

"But someone has been here," said Jayne. "Look! There's paper in the typewriter!"

Charlotte walked forward again and shone her torch on it. She knew what she expected to see. She expected to see "*Spy Quest* by Something Maynard" (what *was* his first name?). Or at least a page of manuscript that needed changing – perhaps he'd discovered another page with Mrs Vormann's name on it, and had to change that as well before he sent it off to the publisher.

But what she did see was quite different. There in the typewriter, the last word half-typed to prove the sudden interruption, were the words:

My name is Mabel Elliott. Born in
this house, April 19th 1859. Murdered
here, midnight July 19th 1886.
Battered to death by the Woman in Bla—

Slowly, Charlotte turned, horror written in her eyes as clear as words in a book, and stared at Miss Gould. Their accomplice stood in the shadows, and for once she wasn't smiling. Charlotte slowly raised a hand to her mouth and suppressed a scream. She caught her breath and a little stifled groan came out instead.

"What is it?" said Jayne. "Charlotte, what is it?"

"Charlotte, what's the matter?" from Miss Gould.

"Have a look at the typewriter, Ben," said Boff. "You're nearest."

Ben went over and read the words. The others, including Miss Gould, crowded over his shoulder. Charlotte had turned away and was spewing words as if she was possessed of an evil spirit.

"Battered to death by the Woman in *Black*!" she gurgled. "That's what she was going to type! We stopped her! Ben! Today's July the 19th! It was typed by her ghost!" Charlotte spun again, riveting her gaze on Miss Gould. "*And the Woman in Black is here*!"

Mr Maynard fell into a large armchair. He was hot from conducting the CD player through no less than four stirring symphonies. His throat was hoarse from singing, his legs were tired from dancing – but he was deliriously happy.

His eyes wandered to the package on the mantelpiece, all wrapped up and ready to go to the publishers. How close he had come! How close!

But now everything was wonderful! Wonderful! As soon as the package was delivered, he would be free from guilt forever! Free! Free! Free!

150

He had better not waste any more time.

He took the package down from the shelf and laid it on the desk. His fingers plucked at the layers of sticky tape that were wrapped round its end, pulling them off. He tugged at the two edges of the opening, forcing the staples apart, and carefully reached inside. He pulled out a new folder. It had typed on it "*Spy Quest* by Michael J Maynard." And on the first sheet inside it repeated the title and was followed by "Chapter One. The Death Papers" and half a page of words that he had retyped on Mrs Vormann's typewriter. The 'o's and 'p's and little 'e's weren't filled in on the retyped page, like they were on the others, but that had never bothered him. He wished he hadn't destroyed the original sheet, but he hadn't felt safe while it existed.

Now he would have to do it all over again. For her sake.

He took the bundle of sheets – five hundred of them – from the folder, and placed them inside a new, unlabelled one. Taking it with him, he moved into the hall, turned off all the lights, put on his black coat, and slipped out into the night.

It was nearing midnight, and he shivered as he walked, feet turned inwards, leaning forwards. He fingered the key in his coat pocket.

Toby finished driving the second screw home, and stood up from his crouching position. The Igmopong had gone in, all four of them, and his task was half done. He lifted the fence panels that they had come through earlier, and ducked through to Pigmo Island. The tent lay glowing further along. He took quick strides towards it and opened the zip. There was food inside. Food in boxes, food in tins, drinks, cream cakes, chocolates. He scooped them all together into two of the boxes, dropped them over the fence into the Sea of Debris, and zipped up the tent again.

He went back through the loose panels, collected the boxes and carried them to Mr Elliott's back door. His foot kicked at something in the darkness and he had to skip to keep his balance. He put the boxes down and shone his torch. It was a tin of red paint lying on its side. He moved it out of the long grass so no one else could trip on it in the night, and placed it next to the fence. Did Ben leave the yellow one there, as well?

Then a picture came into his mind. As he had stooped, for more than half an hour, waiting for the Igmopong, his eyes had grown very accustomed to the dark. He had seen shapes, outlines, silhouettes. His mind recalled a cylindrical shadow with a shiny rim picked out by the crescent moon, lying at an angle under a bush nearby.

He climbed through the fence again, towards the front of Cedric Morgan's house this time, towards where he had lain in wait. Crouching down, he shone his torch so that it was shielded from everything else by his body, and the only thing illuminated was the shadowy cylinder.

It was the tin of yellow paint. Next to it, half buried in the soil, was a paintbrush with yellow paint on it.

At last, Toby knew what they had done. Without hesitating, he clicked off his torch and ran out of Cedric's front garden. He crossed the road at an angle, and entered the black woods.

"This is just a silly joke," said Miss Gould. She pulled the piece of paper from the typewriter. Her torch flitted around the desk, then her smile suddenly radiated again as she turned and tried to cheer everybody up. "Don't upset yourself, Charlotte. There's no Woman in Black, or if there ever was, it's certainly not me."

"But there was no one here! You saw for yourself!"

"Never mind. Forget it. Let's just go upstairs and have our midnight feast." Now she was winking at them.

"But we heard the typing!" said Jayne. "We did. Honestly. Didn't you hear it?"

152

"Come on. There's nothing to be done here."

Miss Gould shepherded them from the room and closed the door. Once outside, she put a finger to her lips. She gathered the four heads towards her own and whispered as quietly as she could, "Don't say anything!" and then led them up the stairs.

"What's going on?" said Boff when they were back in Mr Elliott's bedroom with the door firmly closed. "You know something, don't you?"

"I didn't get into MI5 for nothing," said Miss Gould modestly.

Cedric Morgan crouched on the steps that led up from Mr Elliott's cellar. His face radiated happiness in the dark, and he could sense the suppressed sniggers of Doris, Andy and Amanda who sat on the few steps below him.

"They've gone upstairs," he said at last, quietly chuckling. "Charlotte was really *frightened*, wasn't she?"

"We can get her tomorrow," said Doris. "Who was afraid of a silly old ghost, then?"

"Shall I do it again?" said Cedric. "Or wait a bit?"

"Give 'em a few minutes to start eating."

"I'll load the next bit of paper."

Cedric raised himself through the trap-door in the cupboard floor, holding a sheet of paper that he had kept flat in a folder. He pushed open the door of the cupboard, being careful not to make any noise, waited for his eyes to adjust, then crept towards the stack of furniture. He wriggled his way under some chairs and a small table and found himself face to face with the desk. He switched on his torch and held it under his armpit, trying to keep it pointed towards the typewriter. He carefully wound in the sheet, positioned it so that the last unfinished word was opposite the hammers, and let down the bail to keep it in place on the cylinder. Then he crept back the way he had come, closed the cupboard door,

153

settled on the top step, and raised his hand towards the power switch.

He pulled the switch down, and the cassette player that he had hidden under the desk burst into life.

"Tap, tap, tap-tap, tap, tap, tap, tap-tap-tap, ting!"

He laughed breathlessly in the darkness. It was so clever, and so funny, and it had hooked the silly old Naitabals properly. He had sneaked in during the day with the cassette recorder and done lots and lots of typing – half an hour or more – enough to play it back for half the night. It sounded loudly in the room now.

"Tap-tap-tap, tap-tap, tap-tap, tap, tap, tap-tap, ting!"

He felt his sister and the others huddle closer to listen as a floorboard creaked upstairs.

"They're coming down again!" he whispered. Then his ears strained to listen, his finger poised on the electricity switch. If he crouched at the right level he could see under the cupboard door, under the furniture, and under the door of the front room. He could see torchlight dancing there now.

"Tap-tap, tap-tap, tap..."

He threw the switch off, and the eerie sound of typing stopped instantly. The front room door rushed open, and now there were voices again.

"See!" Charlotte's voice. "There's no one here, and we all heard the typing this time!"

"And there's another piece of paper." Ben's voice.

There was the whirr of the carriage as the paper was pulled out, then Ben's voice again.

"'Murdered by Lady in Black. She smiled a lot, and she looked so nice, but—'"

Cedric had to suppress another fit of laughter, and his fingers dug into the top of his sister's shoulder. He felt her head shaking helplessly against his knee.

He had to admit it was brilliant. He'd seen the silly woman in black going into the Naitabals' tree-house, and

154

that was what had given him the idea. But he couldn't hear Charlotte screaming or anything this time.

"Look!" The woman's voice.

"It's a cassette player!" Boff's voice.

"Do you mean to tell me..." Charlotte's, trailing off.

Now there were footsteps and shufflings.

"Where does the lead go to?"

Suddenly, Cedric realised they were in imminent danger.

"I've found it. Look! It goes over there!"

Cedric signalled with urgent shoves that he needed to move down the steps to close the trap-door, and he felt the weight of bodies beneath him shifting. He inched down another step, then another, pulling the trap-door down over his head as he went.

The shuffling of knees in the room above had changed to footsteps again, and traces of torchlight flitted under the cupboard door and through the cracks.

"It goes into the cupboard!" The woman's voice.

The Igmopong retreated rapidly towards the window that led out on to Mr Elliott's side path, the way they had come in. It showed as a square of dark grey light, and they all made for it as quickly and silently as they could, across the dampness, hands jostling bodies in the rush. Doris reached it first and gave it a push. It didn't budge. She pushed harder.

"It's stuck!" she hissed.

"Let me try!" An urgent whisper from Cedric.

Now they heard the cupboard door being opened; heard the scritch-scratch of fingers exploring the plug where the recorder was plugged in; heard a click and "tap-tap, tap-tap, tap, ting!" as the tape burst into life in the room above; another click as it died again.

"There's a trap-door!" The woman again.

Cedric pushed and pushed at the window, but it wouldn't budge. Then they froze as the trap-door slowly opened, torchlight flooded in, shining yellow off the damp brick

155

floor, reached their startled faces. The beam of a single torch picked them out one by one, each of them poised like a tree in a petrified forest.

Then, just as they were ready for the hand of wrath to descend, a surprising thing happened. The torch went off, and the woman's voice was heard again.

"There's nothing down there."

They couldn't believe their luck. The trap-door was lowered, the bolt was shot across, the cupboard door was closed and locked, and the sounds of the search party receded.

The Igmopong stood for another few moments without moving.

"She – she *saw* us, but she's letting us go!" stuttered Cedric.

"Why would she do that?" said Amanda.

"Yeah..." said Andy.

Then Doris exploded, her voice hoarse with indignation.

"They've locked us in, that's what they've done!" she screamed. "This window was *loose* before! Now it's *solid*!"

"We can break it," said Cedric lamely.

"*It's got bars on it, you brainless lump*! Are you blind as well as stupid, or what?"

Cedric threw himself against the window frame and attacked it in a frenzy of frustration. It still didn't budge.

He paused, waiting for inspiration.

Inspiration came.

"HE-L-L-L-L-P!!"

156

CHAPTER SEVENTEEN

Dangerous Harry

"I wonder where Toby's got to?" said Charlotte, feeling a lot better now that the "ghost" had been well and truly exorcised.

"Yes, he should be back by now," said Jayne.

"I hope he managed to screw up the window all right," said Boff. "We pre-drilled the holes and tested it when the Igmopong were indoors, so it should've been okay."

The four Naitabals and Miss Gould were seated in a circle on the floor of Mr Elliott's bedroom, with Jayne and Charlotte's midnight feast spread before them.

"Perhaps he's still trying to find the Igmopong's food," said Boff.

"Did any of you hear a cry for help just then?" said Miss Gould, smiling as usual.

They all listened. It came from below, distant and muffled.

"HE-L-L-L-L-P!!"

"No, I didn't hear anything," said Charlotte. "Did you, Ben?"

"What?" said Ben. "That cry for help just now? No, I didn't hear it..."

"Nor me," said Jayne.

"Me, neither" said Boff.

"Well!" said Miss Gould brightly, "the tape recorder is unplugged, the murdered ghost of Mabel Elliott has been put finally to rest, and it just remains for me to take that little trip to Mr Maynard's house and—"

She was interrupted by the sound of the back door creaking open.

"There's Toby!" said Ben. "Now we can have the feast!"

Charlotte and Jayne opened the bottles of bat's blood and elderberry crush and poured them out into glasses.

"Would you like a mouse pie Miss Gould?" said Jayne.

Miss Gould was taken aback by the tails and the ears, but she laughed when Jayne told her they were only mince pies with tails and ears made out of liquorice.

"Toby hasn't come up the stairs," said Ben, getting up. "Perhaps he needs help with the Igmopong food."

And then, instead of hearing Toby's footsteps ascending the stairs, they heard the eerie sound again.

"Tap, tap, tap-tap-tap, tap-tap-tap, tap-tap, ting!"

Everyone stopped what they were doing and listened.

"Why's Toby typing?" said Jayne, wrinkling her nose.

"Perhaps it isn't Toby," said Boff, looking serious. "But it can't be the Igmopong. They're snookered, and we've unplugged the cassette player."

Miss Gould rose and beckoned the others to follow. For the third time that night, the procession crept down the stairs, all knowing by this time where the squeaky floorboards were, and avoiding them. Again they stood outside the front room door, and again their torches clicked on, five of them, as Miss Gould pushed open the door.

The typewriter stopped, but this time they all stared into the very surprised face of Mr HMS *Slugface* Maynard.

"I can explain everything," he said, lamely.

Miss Gould stepped forward.

"I'll take that manuscript," she said.

"Oh, I brought it back. I was retyping the first page, you see—"

She snatched it off the desk while HMS *Slugface*, looking very un-slugface-like, cowered on one side.

"Is this the original, girls?" she said, showing it to Jayne and Charlotte.

"That's it," said Jayne. "All the 'o's and 'p's and little 'e's

158

are filled in. Except the first page, of course."

"Yes," said Miss Gould, grimly. "The first page with '*by Michael R Maynard*' written on it!"

"I can explain!" said Mr Maynard again. "Look! It's in the typewriter! I've started re-typing it!"

They all looked. Sure enough, the sheet in the typewriter already said "*Spy Quest* by Hermine Vormann. Chapter One. The Death Papers", and the first few lines had been typed as well.

"*He-l-l-l-l-p!*"

"Did you hear that?" said Mr Maynard.

"What?" said the others.

"*He-l-l-l-l-p!*"

"That," said Mr Maynard.

"No," said the others.

"It came from down there," said Mr Maynard, pointing towards the cupboard in the shadows.

"It's just the ghost of Mabel Elliott," said Jayne, with a perfectly straight face. She raised her voice in the hope that the Igmopong could hear. "She was murdered in the cellar at midnight on July 19th 1886, and her screams can always be heard at midnight on the same day."

"But she's quite harmless," added Charlotte.

While Mr Maynard was looking intrigued and mystified, the back door opened again. Footsteps sounded in the hallway, and Toby appeared at the door, carrying two big boxes. He seemed surprised to see them all downstairs, and especially surprised to see Mr Maynard with them. He was also anxious to convey some news of his own. He was out of breath, he was dishevelled, and he was grinning.

"Where have you been?" said Boff.

"Let's have some grub, and I'll tell you," he panted.

Upstairs again, there were seven in the circle. It was just as well that the circle was bigger, because there was even more food to put into it, thanks to the raid on the Igmopong tent.

"They won't be needing it now," said Toby.

Mr Maynard had been invited to join them, not because anyone actually liked him, but because they were all starving hungry and couldn't wait for explanations before getting started.

"Have some slugs on toast," said Jayne.

"How about a nice cream meringue?"

"Or a crunchy beetle sandwich?"

"Spider delight?"

For a while there was the sound of munching, and crunching, and chewing. Every now and then there were exclamations of delight or disgust as each new dish was brought forth, and great explanations as to how they were made to look so realistic and taste so... so intriguing, as Miss Gould put it.

"Where did you go, Toby?" said Boff at last.

"Let's put it this way," said Toby. "How would you like to spend a week in Cedric's rubber boat?"

"What??"

"Yes. I tripped up Ben's tin of red paint on the way in, much earlier—"

"So did I," said Ben. "I meant to put them back."

"That's just it," said Toby. "It wasn't 'them', it was 'it'."

"What do you mean?"

"There was only one tin there. The yellow tin was in Cedric's front garden."

"You mean – !"

"You don't mean – ?"

"I do. Cedric pinched another chair from under the tarpaulin and painted it yellow. The yellow chair we hid in the woods is still hanging up in the tree. That's where I've been – to check!"

A great cheer went up, and everyone leaned across to slap

Toby on the back.

"Good old Toby!"

"Three cheers for Toby!"

"Now we won't have to give up the tree-house for a week!"

"Hooray!"

"And now," said Miss Gould, "I think it's time we had an explanation from Mr Maynard. Don't you, Naitabals?"

All eyes turned towards Naitabal Enemy Number One. He hadn't seemed at all ominous in the fading torchlight, partly because he had a Cheshire-size grin stretching all the way from one shining ear to the other, and partly because he kept breaking out into little songs, and conducting himself while singing them. As he finished each one he would take a mouthful of food and then break into a series of giggles.

"I," he began, after singing another little song, "have written forty-nine novels..."

"We know," said Jayne. "And my mum said none of them have ever been published."

"And your mother," said Mr Maynard, "is a well-informed lady. Yes – I have written forty-nine novels, and none of them have been published. So I decided to make my fiftieth novel a *tour de force*, a *force majeure*, my *magnum opus*..."

"He means 'a good one'," translated Miss Gould.

"Yes – would anyone like to hear another little song? No? Well, perhaps later... I sat at my desk, gazing out into the garden, waiting for inspiration. Thoughts went round and round in my brain.

"The trouble, of course, is the publishers – they rarely recognise great talent like mine." Another series of giggles. "One of them even had the cheek to say that I couldn't write! Had I ever considered sending my manuscript to a recycling plant? I recycled his letter instead.

"But for two weeks, no ideas or words came for my fiftieth novel. And then my next door neighbour, Mrs Vormann, telephoned. She wasn't well, and would I call an ambulance and go and see her. I always told her to ring me if she felt ill – I could get there quickly. I called the ambulance. She'd had the presence of mind to open her front door, but when I arrived she was lying on the floor by the telephone, unconscious. I made her comfortable until help arrived and they took her to hospital. I stayed behind to tidy up. That was when I saw her manuscript. It was on the desk, and the secret drawer where she must have kept it was open. She'd been making a few handwritten changes, I think.

"I started to read it, and I was gripped. The writing was fresh, crisp and exciting. It was a spy story, and it was so good that I believed everything in it must really have happened. It grabbed my attention from the very first page. My mind flowed through the narrative like a swift running stream, taking me down, down, out on to a sea of discovery, and to the distant continent of its magnificent ending..."

"He liked it," translated Miss Gould.

"Another little song, yet, anyone? No? Never mind....

"I found it incredible that such a book could have been written by a modest old lady of ninety-two, but there it was. I read it again, enjoyed it just as much – almost more than the first time.

"And suddenly, everything I had ever written seemed worthless by comparison. I felt mad with jealousy, that this dear old lady of ninety-two could write something so brilliant, so effortlessly, and yet I – I had struggled through forty-nine books, and all for nothing –

"It appeared she had had a heart attack. But the next day she was on the telephone from the hospital. She sounded very weak. Had I put the manuscript away? I assured her I had. It was important that it was hidden, she said. I said I was sorry, but I'd been unable to stop reading it. Had she considered sending it to a publisher? No. Not until after her death. Had anyone else read it? No. A few days later she had another heart attack and died peacefully in her sleep."

"So you switched the manuscript in Mr Elliott's van, and you came here to retype the first page with *your name* on it," said Miss Gould. "A shameful thing to do. Making people believe that you had written it, and not Mrs Vormann."

Mr Maynard hung his head.

"Yes." Then he raised his head again and burst into maniacal laughter. He reached inside his coat pocket and produced a piece of paper. "But then I got this!"

He threw the piece of paper into the air, stood up, and started dancing round the circle, in and out, just missing the food and the hands and the feet, and in the end everyone was laughing.

Miss Gould retrieved the sheet of paper when he passed her the second time round, and scanned it.

"A publisher has accepted your forty-ninth book!" she said.

"Yes, yes, yes, yes, yes, yes, yes, YES!" sang Mr Maynard. "But I only got the letter this morning! It had been delivered on Saturday to the wrong house, and a child – a little child—"

"Me and Harry..." said Charlotte.

" – brought it round today!"

"And so you came back. You came back to type the page again with Mrs Vormann's name..."

"Yes, yes, yes, yes, yes, yes, YES! And leave it there in the secret drawer for Mr Elliott to find! So I'm a nice man after all! Aren't I a nice man after all, children?"

He was still being slimy, so no one really trusted him, but they couldn't help smiling at each other as he danced by for the eighth time.

In the end, Charlotte and Jayne decided to return to the Naitabal hut with the others after the midnight feast.

"We don't want to be kept up half the night with pitiful

cries of help from the cellar," Jayne had said, without emotion. "It'll serve them right for pinching our food and cheating in the Great Chair Hunt."

"How did Harry get my bow and arrow?" said Charlotte. It was morning, and she was looking from the west window at her little brother two gardens away, who was loosing off arrows in random directions. "I'll strangle him when I get hold of him."

"We'll have to get our chair down today," said Ben. "We can't leave it where it is, polluting the countryside."

"And we can explore Jungle Island," said Boff.

"Yes," said Charlotte. "We shouldn't have so much trouble crossing Slug Island now."

"Miss Gould is going to send the manuscript back in a day or two, when they've changed all the names," said Charlotte. "Then Boff can send it to his aunt."

"I hope she gets it published."

"Bound to, if it's as good as Mr Maynard said it was."

"Nearly ten o'clock," said Jayne. "It's time to let the Igmopong out, and get their rubber boat."

"Harry!" Charlotte clenched a fist at the window, then half turned to the others. "He's just put one of my arrows into Cedric Morgan's tent." She opened the trap-door, poked her head out upside down, and shouted. "Harry! Stop firing those arrows!"

"Tentbang!" shouted Harry.

"Oh dear, there's no hope, is there?" murmured Charlotte.

At ten o'clock exactly, five Naitabals were clustered round the little pit where the window to Mr Elliott's cellar was set in.

Toby, roused early for the occasion, undid the two screws that held the window firmly shut, and then eased it open. The sight that met their eyes was not a pleasant one.

The four Igmopong were huddled in a group on the steps, half-lying and half-sitting, trying to keep themselves off the

164

cold, damp floor.

"We wondered where you were," said Toby. "This window seems to have got stuck, but we've loosened it now."

"It's ten o'clock," said Cedric. His mind was still in a roseate dream, in spite of a cold, sleepless night and aching all over. "We can have your tree-house now."

"No, you can't," said Toby.

"What?"

"Why not?" said Doris, even more belligerent after a night of discomfort. She struggled free of the tangle of limbs and bodies and steps, and came towards them slowly, half doubled up with cramp.

"Because I found this," said Toby.

The four Igmopong blinked at the pot of yellow paint in the bright light of the window, and knew straight away that they were beaten.

"And that means we can have your rubber boat for a week instead," said Ben.

Doris turned away again, grim faced, to begin the process of hanging, drawing and quartering her brother. His first scream, however, was drowned by a loud explosion from Pigmo Island.

"Oh, no! Harry's hit your boat with one of my arrows!" shouted Charlotte.

And from the distance, carried on the cold morning air, came Harry's scream of laughter:

"Boat... BANG!"

CHAPTER EIGHTEEN

Postscript

Two days later, in an office, somewhere in London, a secretary is complaining.

"Are you sure this is what you want to say?" she says. She looks through her spectacles at the handwritten letter. "It's not your usual style *at all*."

"Yes," says her boss. Her boss is dressed in a black suit, and she is smiling.

The secretary types the letter. It is headed "FOR NAITABAL EYES ONLY" and it says:

> How are you all? Unfortunately I am without my car right now. It is having its brakes done. Of course, it would have to be today! I couldn't contact you earlier because I have been away. Telephone me any time. As for helping with all the preparations for the lovely slug sandwiches – thanks! Did I eat too many?"

The secretary adds the boss's name and hands the typed letter to her boss for checking.

"You don't think it's a bit *stilted*?" she asks.

"No, that's perfect, thank you. And when you post it, it *must* have four twopenny stamps on the envelope – and no more – and one threepenny stamp. The rest must be made up with pennies. Can you *promise* me you will do that?"

The secretary looks at her boss as if she is quite mad.

"Yes, Miss Gould."

"Thank you," says Miss Gould. "I do believe it's one of the best letters I've ever written."

There are now six books in
David Schutte's Naitabal Mystery series.

If you enjoyed this book, you'll love the others!

1. DANGER, KEEP OUT!
ISBN 1-904028-00-4   £5.00

Miss Coates steamed up the garden path. Her white hair glowed in the moonlight. She stopped at the well in the middle of her lawn, and shone her torch into it. And then... she disappeared.

   To ordinary people, she's Miss Coates, but to the Naitabals she's the old enemy battleship, the SS *Coates*. And she's hiding something. Why has she grown huge hedges around her garden, so no one can see into it? And why is she so desperate to stop anyone snooping?
   Determined to discover the truth, the Naitabals go investigating. But the secrets they uncover lie deep in the past - a past that Miss Coates will do anything to conceal...

"Get ready for an invasion of wild ten-year-olds... "
The Daily Telegraph

There are now six books in
David Schutte's Naitabal Mystery series.

If you enjoyed this book, you'll love the others!

3. WILD WOODS, DARK SECRET
ISBN 1-904028-02-0   £5.00

*The woman was moving along a track a little way above
them.   Instead of walking, she seemed to be sailing
effortlessly, floating like a ghost above the ground...*

  The Naitabal gang are promised the holiday of a lifetime at
Mr Blake's remote country house. But from the very first
moment, their visit is plunged into mystery.
  Why has Mr Blake disappeared? What is the meaning of
the weird coded messages? Who are the sinister strangers
that prowl the dark, forbidding woods?
  Only one thing is clear – Mr Blake is in big trouble...

*"The Naitabals are a wild species of human aged about 10 who
inhabit these great books... I hope David Schutte can keep adding
to the series... "*
The School Librarian

There are now six books in
David Schutte's Naitabal Mystery series.

If you enjoyed this book, you'll love the others!

4. BEHIND LOCKED DOORS

ISBN 1-904028-03-9   £5.00

The message was written in purple ink on yellow paper.   In an almost illegible spidery scrawl, it said...
'PLEASE HELP ME!'

  Mrs Hooper has not left her home or spoken to anyone for twenty years, ever since her husband died. His hat, coat and umbrella still hang in the hall, untouched, covered in dust.
  Now the Naitabals realise she might be in trouble. What sinister secrets are hidden within Mrs Hooper's spooky old house? Why has she locked herself away for so long? When the Naitabals finally open the locked doors, they find a mystery far more evil than any of them could have imagined...

"Have you got a Naitabal in your garden?   According to author David Schutte, a Naitabal is 'a wild species of human aged about ten', it feeds on 'anything, except what its parents want it to' and it lives mainly in tree-houses. If your own Naitabal hankers for ... adventure, buy it one of Schutte's Naitabal Mysteries."
The Times

There are now six books in
David Schutte's Naitabal Mystery series.

If you enjoyed this book, you'll love the others!

5. GHOST ISLAND
ISBN 1-904028-05-5   £5.00

The house that was Ghost Island was silhouetted against the sky, towering above the lake. Thick, round wooden posts stuck up out of the water a few metres from it, like giant hippo teeth, encircling the whole house as far as their eyes could see.

When the Naitabals see the unusual advertisement in their local newspaper, they know they won't rest until they can unravel its strange meaning:

```
       He/she who solves this
          exquisite puzzle
     should use the digits below
         to check if it fits.
              186945
```

Its solution leads them to Ghost Island – and to a mystery that has remained unsolved for fourteen years.

It's the Naitabals' biggest challenge yet.

"Have you got a Naitabal in your garden? According to author David Schutte, a Naitabal is 'a wild species of human aged about ten', it feeds on 'anything, except what its parents want it to' and it lives mainly in tree-houses. If your own Naitabal hankers for … adventure, buy it one of Schutte's Naitabal Mysteries."

The Times

There are now six books in
David Schutte's Naitabal Mystery series.

If you enjoyed this book, you'll love the others!

6. DEAD MAN'S CHEST

ISBN 1-904028-06-3   £5.00

It was a light oak box strengthened with metal straps like a pirate's treasure chest. The edges of the lid were decorated with silhouettes of pirate figures burnt into the wood. Charlotte read the message branded on the lid across the middle: 'SARAH'S LITTLE TREASURE'.

The Naitabals have never seen a living soul at the lonely Deep Shadow Cottage in Gray's Wood. But when Jayne catches a glimpse of a face at the window, it heralds a chain of events that plunge even the woods themselves into danger.

Who really owns the cottage? How did a burning house link its tenant with a past cloaked in mystery?

The fifteen pirates burnt into the lid of the dead man's little wooden chest are just one of the clues that lead the Naitabals to the stunning secret.

"Have you got a Naitabal in your garden? According to author David Schutte, a Naitabal is 'a wild species of human aged about ten', it feeds on 'anything, except what its parents want it to' and it lives mainly in tree-houses. If your own Naitabal hankers for … adventure, buy it one of Schutte's Naitabal Mysteries."
The Times